Campbell Geeslin

THE BONNER BOYS

A Novel about Texans

SIMON AND SCHUSTER

NEW YORK

Published by Simon and Schuster
A Division of Gulf & Western Corporation
Simon & Schuster Building
Rockefeller Center
1230 Avenue of the Americas
New York, New York 10020

SIMON AND SCHUSTER and colophon are trademarks of Simon & Schuster
Designed by Eve Kirch
Manufactured in the United States of America

1   3   5   7   9   10   8   6   4   2

Library of Congress Cataloging in Publication Data

Geeslin, Campbell.
The Bonner boys.
I. Title.
PS3557.E352W5   813'.54   80–27400
ISBN 0–671–42430–0

Contents

Author's Note

This novel is for my family—past, present and future. When I was growing up I liked to tap dance and tell long stories. My mother would interrupt with, "Now, son! You know you're stretching the truth." And that's just what I've done in this book. I've stretched every truth until none of the people or places bears any resemblance to the real thing. If the names or descriptions of any character suggest any real person that is an accident and not my intention. This is a work of fiction and the events and conversations recounted here never took place. My brothers didn't like my tap dancing so I gave it up. I didn't want to disgrace them. Storytelling has turned out to be a lot harder to give up.

A Brief Prelude

THEY were up on the stage with the lights shining in their faces. Banyan said later he felt as if they were on exhibit, freaks in some kind of traveling sideshow. Flannel suddenly wondered if Horner had zipped his fly shut. He was always forgetting it.

It was one of their father's luncheon club nights. The club had these programs to raise money for worthy town projects. The man who was the entertainment that evening had come to town highly recommended by the Brownwood Rotary. He called himself Mr. Mental. He started off his program with a string of jokes. Just about the time he told his third one, Flannel felt his mother freeze in her seat beside him so he began to listen, figuring that what Mr. Mental was saying must be dirty. The men in the audience were going haw, haw, haw. Keel was poking Field in the ribs, but Flannel decided he must be too young to understand the drift of the jokes.

Mr. Mental had on a black coat with tails hanging down the back. He played the piano and sang Irish ballads in a high whine. When he sat down at the high school's old upright, he flipped up those tails on his coat. Flannel's mother didn't like his joke telling, but she said on the way home that he certainly was graceful the way he could flip his tails with just a quick little gesture. Those two black strips of coat floated up like a soaring buzzard's wings, twitched and then settled back down over the edge of the bench.

Could Flannel actually remember seeing him do that? Or was it Flannel's mother's telling the story over and over again through the years that made him think he remembered everything so clearly?

Flannel did remember the painful embarrassment of being up on that stage. The man had asked for volunteers for his next stunt. There weren't any. Then Panky Frinet said in a loud voice, "Thomas, why don't you send those boys of yours up there?" There was laughter and clapping, and right behind Flannel some girls giggled.

Thomas Bonner said in a low voice, "All right. Why don't you boys go up and help us out on this?"

Keel stood and started to the front. The stage was set up in the gym whenever anyone wanted to use the place as an auditorium. The other four boys followed Keel, up a little ladderlike set of steps onto the platform stage.

Flannel's friend Billy Boy Ellie began laughing like a nanny goat. Flannel could feel the heat in his face, so he knew that it was bright red. Flannel used to die inside when his mother got up to sing in church, which was practically every Sunday. He certainly never had any desire to exhibit himself in front of an audience. In the first place, he was chronically self-conscious. He was skinny. "That Bonner boy's little arms look like twigs," people would say, right out loud so Flannel could hear them.

The five boys lined up on the stage like stairsteps. Keel at seventeen was almost full grown, over six feet tall. Field was only a little shorter. Banyan came next. Then Flannel. He was nine years old. That would make it 1932. Horner was almost five.

Mr. Mental had asked for volunteers so he could show off his fortune-telling abilities. He started at the short end of the line with Horner. At that time Horner had blond curls all over his head. That hair was a source of friction in the family for years. Keel thought it ought to be cut off. Their mother didn't. He was her baby, her last one. Horner did have pretty hair, just like the angels on a Christmas greeting card.

What the man came up with on that stage was somewhat uncanny, Flannel recalled. But Flannel was not at all sure, on the other hand, that time hadn't done some clever editing. Maybe Mr. Mental was one of those people who can size up strangers at first meeting, can make shrewd guesses just by observing a person closely.

He patted Horner on the head. "Well, young man, what's your name?"

"Horner Bonner." Horner spoke right up in a loud, clear voice that got a nice laugh from the audience.

"Horner? You mean like in Little Jack Horner sat in the corner?"

Poor Horner. He's gotten that same stupid question asked that same way all his life. On this night, for the first time, he said, "Yes, sir, but I never ate a plum pie."

Well, the audience just laughed like fools at that, and their father was laughing the loudest of all. Their mother said later she thought Horner sounded like a smarty-pants, but Horner had said it seriously, and he was surprised when the audience laughed so hard. Their approval gave him even more confidence. Flannel looked down and saw that Horner's fly was closed, which eased Flannel's mind. Mr. Mental asked, "Well, Horner, what do you want to be when you grow up?"

Horner said, "You're the fortune-telling man. You tell me."

Even their mother had to laugh at that fast piece of back talk.

And Mr. Mental laughed, too. Flannel didn't like seeing the man up close. His face was dark and heavily lined with unexpected gullies. His eyes darted, fast as a snake's tongue. He spun out a long-winded tale about how Horner would want to be an actor on the stage, but he would not do that and would use his talents instead to become a lawyer with a silver tongue who would win many important law cases in court.

Flannel was next. The man had sharp little teeth that were brown. He gave off a strong medicinal odor. He said, "Well, this one is the last one to get to the table, isn't he?" Flannel turned red again at the laughing. "What's your name?"

Flannel had to clear his throat. "Flannel Bonner."

"Flannel?"

Flannel nodded.

"Flannel—like in a piece of cloth?"

"It's my mama's mama's last name. I'm named for my grandmother," Flannel explained in misery. He was sure everybody in the audience already knew him and where he got his name. He felt like an idiot.

The man said, "Well, Flannel, I don't think you're going to become a great prizefighter when you grow up. But I think you're going to go far, however—far away from Texas and live in a big city where you work in a skyscraper building." He shut his eyes. "I can't see what kind of work it is, but you'll do all right."

The audience applauded, but Flannel's future struck him as just plain awful. He always felt as if he got the most mediocre fortune of the lot, as it turned out.

Mr. Mental, of course, made a remark about Banyan's red hair and how none of the boys really looked much like brothers, which they had all heard often enough. Everyone in town was always saying that. The man told Banyan he was going to be an artist. Banyan, who had already gotten serious about the piano, said, "I'm not going to paint pictures. I can't draw at all."

"Oh, no," the man said quickly. "I didn't mean that kind of artist." He shut his eyes and held his hand over Banyan's head. "I see writing poetry and playing music. I think it's playing music that you'll be doing."

Well, everyone just applauded like crazy when Mr. Mental said that because Banyan had been playing at the church for years. Everyone knew he was interested in music, and there was just no way a stranger from out of town could have known such a thing.

The man told Field that he would be a cowboy or a sheriff, which was a surprise to everyone and got some laughs. Field wore thick glasses. And the glasses, Field once explained to Flannel, made him look smart—but he was smart, too.

Keel's fortune got the biggest audience reaction of all. Keel was handsome and knew it. It didn't take much fortune-telling ability for the man to say that Keel was going to know many beautiful women in his life. Keel already was being chased by half the girls in the county, and he was chasing the other half. Their mother was disgusted, she said later. She said the man made Keel sound like a Don Juan.

Mr. Mental added that he could see Keel living for many years in a far-off country where the people spoke a different language. He said that Keel would become very, very rich. That got some clapping and one of Keel's friends yelled, "Can I borrow two bits off you, Keel?"

The boys filed off the platform after that, and Flannel slunk back to his seat next to his mother, mortified at having his pitiful skinniness pointed out in public.

In the car going home, their father thanked them for cooperating and said that they were certainly the best part of the program. Their mother hugged Flannel because she knew he was miserable, and she lectured Horner about the dangers of becoming a show-off. Banyan said the man was a terrible pianist, and his fortune-telling probably was just as poor.

Gradually that evening became one of their mother's stock stories that could be triggered with, "You remember the time the fortune-telling man got all the boys up on the stage?"

The next week, or soon after, Keel went off to the university. Oh, there must have been a few more holidays when all the boys were home at the same time, but Flannel couldn't remember any. The war came. Keel went first, called up by the navy and sent to the Pacific even before Pearl Harbor. Then Field and Banyan were drafted, and finally Flannel. Only Horner was too young for World War II.

Decades passed.

Except for Field, who went back and took over the weekly newspaper, none of them lived in Lady. Keel liked the taste of foreign life he got in the navy. He went to La Isla, an island country off the coast of South America, and settled down there.

15

ONE

Keel Bonner

O N his way to his office in downtown Puerto Seguro, Keel looked up from his papers just in time to see a girl standing on the curb. She was from the country, her hair in long braids. The rough cotton skirt and blouse were practically a uniform for country girls. But she carried nothing, not even a bag. And she stood erect, motionless, with the morning workers milling around and past her. "Go around the block, Miguel," Keel commanded sharply.

They circled the Sears store and an open market with rows of baskets strung from poles of bamboo and came back to the same corner on the avenida. The girl was still there.

Keel said, "Just pull up in front of her."

Keel opened the door and smiled up at her. "Señorita?"

She looked relieved and slipped in beside him. Her body gave off waves of strong odors, of stale sweat and dank tropical forests.

Miguel turned uncertainly. Keel said to him, "To the office." To the girl he smiled and asked, "What's your name?"

"Milagro." Her voice was soft. Unlike most country girls, she did not giggle or blush. She looked at him directly, inspecting him.

Keel smiled at her, reassuring her, he hoped. He said to Miguel, "Let us off in the back."

Miguel passed the Da Lada Building and turned into the alley behind. There were sleeping men among the trash boxes. Miguel stopped and jumped out to open the rear door for Keel. Milagro got out and Keel followed. He took out his keys and unlocked the door to the building.

Miguel said, "Have a nice day, señor."

Keel nodded and held the door for the girl. They would have to climb three flights up the back stairs, but he couldn't take her up in the elevator. She followed him in silence. He could smell her.

There was no one in the halls. Keel unlocked the door that led directly into his office and held it for the girl. She was inspecting everything. Certainly she wasn't afraid. He pointed to the couch. He went to the door to his waiting room and opened it. Nita was there at her desk. "Good morning, Nita," he said. "I have to have some quiet for a few minutes this morning. No calls until I tell you. All right?"

"Of course, Mr. Bonner. Just flash the telephone when you are ready." Keel nodded to the man who was sitting there in his waiting room. There had been no appointments, but someone was there and he looked familiar. Wasn't he from customs? What in the hell was he doing back so soon, in less than a month? Damn it, didn't he see the photograph of Keel in the paper with el presidente's wife this morning?

Keel shut the door softly and bolted it.

When he turned he saw that Milagro was half reclining on the couch. She had pulled up her skirt and opened her legs. She looked up at him, her face blank. Her eyes were black, enormous. He felt a flush of heat in his upper legs. He smiled at her and began to undress, his heart thudding pleasantly. He hung his jacket and trousers up carefully on the hook on the back of the door.

Ten years earlier, Keel probably would have become totally obsessed by having found such a beautiful and bold new girl. He especially liked her calmness, her lack of interest. She seemed to have a clear sense of herself, a remarkable trait in one so young.

He opened her blouse and found her high breasts were a creamy brown, the nipples coral pink. Afterward, he felt a little embarrassed because his sudden passion had seemed a childish, uncontrolled spasm. She remained still throughout. She watched him as he dressed. Now he could smell her odors on his own body. They would be on him all day. The idea pleased him. As he sat on the edge of his desk to tie his shoes, she closed her blouse and pushed down her skirt. He patted her leg and smiled at her. She stood. She was a tiny little thing.

Keel unlocked the door to the waiting room. "Could you come in a minute, Nita?"

He sat behind his desk. Nita came in with her notebook. She showed no surprise at seeing the girl there. Keel thought perhaps she had heard his noises through the wall. "Nita, this is Milagro. She's the daughter of my caretaker on the ranch up north, and she needs a place to stay. Would you take her around the corner to the Nacional and get her a room? See that she has breakfast, and tell León to give her an inside room on the patio. The street is too noisy."

Nita nodded. "That's Señor García again. He saw the paper this morning. I shoved it under his nose. But still he insists on seeing you. You don't have to kick in again so soon. Watch out for him."

Nita wrinkled her nose and said to Milagro, "Let's go get you in a bathtub, *querida mia.*"

Keel thought that García might be annoyed at having been kept waiting. If so, then Milagro might prove to have been very expensive already. But the man was all smiles and apologies for dropping by without an appointment.

Keel ushered him into his office and, since Nita was gone, left the door open to the waiting room. This made García uneasy.

Keel reassured him. "But we can hear if anyone comes in, and our business is always on the up and up." Under the desk Keel could press his shrunken private parts gently without García seeing what he was doing. The girl truly was a find, a treasure. At lunchtime he would buy her some clothes and spend his siesta with her at the hotel. . . .

García was talking. Keel realized that the man was sweating nervously. Clearly, García had some kind of problem. Keel nodded and smiled encouragingly. García was saying, ". . . it

21

would be an auction of the goods. The documents would show that you bid a hundred and fifty U.S. dollars for the lot. Then I need another hundred and fifty, in U.S. dollars, too," he added softly.

Keel said, "I'm sorry. I guess I didn't understand what you were saying at the beginning. What is it I'm bidding for?"

García looked down. "It is a mixed lot we seized off a boat in the harbor last night. These kids were trying to bring in some hashish. We will burn that, of course. And they had this other cargo. We don't have time to inspect it all thoroughly. I promise you will not lose money on your bid, señor. I am sure a smart man like you, with your friends, may even make a great deal of money." He smiled slyly.

"I'll send Miguel to pick it up. Will it all fit in the trunk of my car?"

"No. But in the back seat and the trunk of your Buick, it will fit." García looked suddenly relieved.

Keel stood. "I'll walk down to the harbor at noon and drop off the money at your office."

"Dollars?"

"Yes, of course. Just as you said."

García said, "I'll have the receipt from the auction all drawn up. It will all be legal. I promise you will have no problem with these goods."

"I'll see you at noon," Keel said. García's promises were ominous. In La Isla when a native said there were no problems, that all would be simple, it meant that there would be impossible complications.

Keel strolled to the bank and took out the cash he needed in dollars. He had been in just the day before to withdraw money for his trip to the States, a business expense. This time he explained it casually to the clerk by saying, "My wife in the States . . ." and shrugged. There were laws about taking dollars out of La Isla. He got an additional six hundred pesetas. He would buy something pretty for Milagro.

Keel walked on down the street past the import shops, the

warehouses, to the water. He stood for a moment looking off the pier at the four ugly, rusting ships in the harbor. It was hot, sultry. Gulls screamed. Workmen on the docks were sitting in the shade of the sheds, eating rolled tortillas and drinking beer. In a minute they would just slump down where they crouched and fall asleep. Siesta. What a nice word. Keel yawned.

He turned and strolled to the customs offices and climbed the wooden steps. Señor García was waiting for him. The ceiling fan barely stirred the hot air.

"The boxes are very heavy, Señor Bonner."

"Miguel will come for them this afternoon. You have someone who can help him load them into the car?"

"Of course, señor."

Keel counted out fifteen twenty-dollar bills. Then he unrolled the pesetas and added a couple of fifty-peseta notes. García counted, too, but politely, barely moving his lips. He nodded as the last bill went down. The fan ruffled the money, and García reached for it before it could blow off the desk. He put it all into a drawer. Then he took some printed forms from a clipboard. "Your papers are in order, señor."

Keel folded them and slipped them into his inside jacket pocket. "Have a nice afternoon," he said. On the wall behind García was a calendar with a color photo of a girl, very blond, in a bikini.

On the way to the Nacional Hotel, Keel stopped off in the Paris Dress Shoppe and bought a white negligee with tiny silk-covered buttons down the front.

At the hotel desk he smiled at the manager and said, "My key, if you please, León." The box under Keel's arm was bright pink.

He rode in the elevator to the third floor and walked along the balcony hallway that overlooked a central patio below. He unlocked the door of room 321. The shutters were closed and Milagro was a soft range of mountains (like those of her homeland, Keel thought poetically) on the bed. Two strips of bright sunlight came in under the shutters. Keel smiled and pinched his nose gently in a gesture that he had turned into habit fifty years ago.

With it he had reshaped a slightly blunt, fat nose into an elegant, aristocratic one.

All the rooms in the Nacional were like this one. All the girls of La Isla were like this one, he thought happily. She sat up as he closed the door behind him. The smell of the tropical countryside, of dank earth and heavy, warm mists, was gone from her body. She smelled like the soap in the hotel. Her pubic hair was a damp, wiry mat that turned into fuzz as it grew up toward her navel. Her belly was a beautiful, beautiful curving surface to be stroked.

Miguel was waiting at the front curb in the Buick, leaning against the front fender, smoking, chattering with another driver. He opened the door in front for Keel. There were two large wooden crates in the backseat area.

Keel asked, "They wouldn't fit in the trunk?" He didn't like to ride in the front next to his driver.

"There is a bigger crate in the trunk, señor. Very heavy. See how the car sits low like a female dog hunched down to piss?"

Keel frowned and climbed in. García had been too kind.

Miguel went around, climbed in, started the motor and drove slowly away from the curb. "It feels like I am driving a hearse with a dead elephant in the back," he joked.

Sometimes Miguel's colorful images made Keel smile, but he was suddenly conscious of the heavy smell in the car. It was oil, of oil on metal. He remembered it from childhood.

His father had kept a shotgun in his closet with the shells in his top bureau drawer. The gun was used when a skunk got after the chickens. But in the fall his father would go out into the west pasture with Keel, a towheaded six-year-old, trotting along beside him. They would crouch down in a clump of live oak in view of the tank, a mud-colored pond at the end of a gully. It was evening. The brown weeds were dusty.

The doves came in from the north, and it wasn't at all unusual for Thomas to hit three or even four birds with a single blast.

Keel acted as dog, watching carefully where the birds fell and running out after each shot to pick them up. Occasionally they

24

were still alive and flopping around so that he would quickly wring each neck. Usually a gray film dropped over their beady little eyes, but Keel didn't like the idea that they might be watching him. He put the tiny heads under a flat stone. The soft, curving breast, warm with life, plump with autumn maize, just fit into the palm of his hand. Later he would hold a girl's breast, cupped in his hand, and remember the soft, warm doves.

By the time he was eight he had begun to beg his father to let him shoot, too. And one day Thomas handed him the big shotgun and said, "Okay. Load it, son. No, keep the muzzle pointed to the ground. Hold it up! Don't let it get any dirt in the barrel."

The shotgun was too heavy. Keel struggled to flip out the empty shell and put in a new one. The barrel was hot from firing. He smelled hot oil and gunpowder. Keel began to sweat from the struggle. Finally the shell was in place and he was ready, his heart thwacking against his ribs. They waited. His father said, "In just a minute now . . . I bet your mama already has the skillet hot for these birds. There's nothing better than fried bird. . . . Do you know how to lead them, son? Sight down the barrel and keep it pointed just in front of the first birds in the bunch. . . ."

Keel's arms were trembling from the weight. He braced his elbow on his knee.

His father said, "I think I hear a bunch coming. . . ." He was crouched just behind Keel, and he helped lift the gun up and position it against the boy's shoulder. Keel could scarcely reach the trigger. He heard the faint whirl of the birds and looked up. He struggled to pull away from his father. "I want to do it, Papa."

His father let go just as the birds swept in. The shotgun's weight pulled it down and as Keel jerked it back up, the gun fired. At first the noise hurt worse than the blow of the stock against his shoulder. The stench of oil and powder was nauseating. Keel was stunned.

When he regained consciousness, his father was holding him. "You got to hold it up firm against your shoulder or it'll kick like a mule. I thought you knew that." The gun oil was on his hands.

The pain in his shoulder was an agony, but he pulled away, out of his father's arms. "Did I get any birds?"

His father let out a burst of laughter. "You'll make a hunter, Keel. Let's go look and see."

Miguel swerved out and around a truck.

Keel couldn't remember now, more than fifty years later, whether or not he had killed any birds on that first shot. But the following Christmas he had been given a thirty-thirty. The rest of the winter he had hunted rabbits with it, skinning them and tanning their hides the way the Indians had, by rubbing ashes into the skins. His mother thought it was disgusting.

Miguel said, "Where are we going to put the boxes, señor?"

"Can you and Pedro lift them?"

Miguel shrugged. "Sí. . . . We can slide them out of the car." He honked at a jitney taxi covered with men hanging on, on their way home from work, too. They shouted obscenities as Miguel passed and the encounter seemed to cheer Miguel. "Sure, we can put them in the garage. With the cars parked there, no one can get them out."

Keel said, "All right. Get Pedro to help you." He was sweating. The air conditioning in the Buick didn't work very well and no one in Puerto Seguro could fix it.

Miguel drove up the circular driveway and let Keel out at the front door. The women, as Keel thought of them, were waiting for him. The door opened and they greeted him with high-pitched cries in Spanish. His wife thought that servants looked smart in pink uniforms. Everyone else in Puerto Seguro put their domestics in white. The pink material was stiff with starch over the plump brown figures. They were short, plump, pink birds, faces turned up to him, chattering.

The women always wanted to know instantly what his plans for the evening were. "I'm going to take a shower, but I want a gin, please. Then dinner at seven." They scattered in all directions.

Keel called out to Pedro who was in the doorway to the kitchen. "Miguel needs help with some boxes in the garage." All the women returned: the housekeeper Dolores, the cook, the maids, the children's amahs were all around him in the entrance hallway, smiling up at him. Why couldn't he get rid of some of them? He was the only one living in this huge house now, and it was overrun with servants. Now even his servants had servants to look after them.

He was handed a crystal glass with a large portion of good Holland gin and a dash of bitters to turn it pink and kill the sweetness. No ice. He had been in La Isla more than thirty years. Ice was for tourists.

He pulled off his jacket and a maid took it from him. "Thank you, Tía," he said. He carried his glass off down the hall, swirling the liquid in it. He would wait until he was in his part of the house alone before he took the first sip.

He put the drink down on top of his bureau and stripped. He hung up his trousers carefully and put the damp shirt and shorts and socks into the hamper. He felt as if he had spent most of his day taking off and putting on clothes. His shorts smelled of the new girl, of sex. He was tired. The gin was a sharp sensation.

On his way to the shower he paused in his exercise room. The man in the full-length mirror was almost trim. Keel liked to see himself in mirrors, even now that he was past sixty. If only his hair weren't so thin . . . He had had blond hair as a young man, and it had just grayed out into a lighter color. His mustache was heavy and full, satisfying to touch, to stroke.

The glass in his hand was expensive. Baccarat, probably. His wife always had the best. She liked things French. She had taken an apartment in San Antonio for the winter now. He shrugged. It was her money. She was very wealthy. He watched himself in the mirror, drinking off the gin. He put the glass on the seat of his stationary bicycle and winked at the dirty old man in the mirrors. In a week or so he would try to teach the new girl how to touch a certain spot with her tongue. Just thinking of that sensation, the feeling that it would bring to him, gave him a moment of warmth, of pleasure. He remembered the pony back home on the ranch, his penis getting bigger, hanging down, swinging.

The bathroom was tiled in brown. Keel himself had designed

the enormous shower closet with its three needle-pointed shower-heads set at different heights. With all of them on, he felt as if he were being pounded from all sides by a hot, steaming tropical rainstorm. It blotted out all other sensations, all thought.

Keel ate dinner sitting alone at the head of the table in the dining room. He felt lonely, but he was never alone. He thought that he had spent his whole life that way. There had been all those little brothers as he was growing up. Now there were servants. He decided he would have Miguel drive him over to Linda's house. He would tell her good-bye, tell his granddaughters a story and put them to bed.

Linda had married a native. Her mother could never forgive that. But who else could Linda have met on La Isla? Linda's husband was a doctor. Her marriage hadn't hurt Keel's business in La Isla at all. Probably it helped. And if Alberto, the president, should suddenly be thrown out of office, Linda's doctor would be all right. Doctors always were.

Keel finished his coffee and lit the one cigar of the day that he allowed himself. The women came and removed all the dishes from the table. He thanked them gravely and stood up.

At the back entrance to the house he flipped on the lights and watched the pool appear, a glowing, rippleless oval of intense blue. The lush plants around the walls were, in the yellowish lights, a piercing shade of green. Keel let himself out and walked across the patio to the door in the wall that opened into the garage. He flipped on more lights.

The Buick, the Ford and the Jeep were in their places. The wooden crates were in front of them against the wall. Keel wondered if he could find a hammer without calling for Miguel. The long box, which had been in the trunk of the Buick, probably held rifles. Or it could even have several of the new light machine guns inside.

Well, García hadn't cheated him. Guns were worth far more than the three hundred he had paid. But selling them would be extremely dangerous. Keel leaned down and sniffed. There was no mistaking the odor. Of course, they might be sewing machines. Keel smiled to himself.

On the way back through the house he paused at the kitchen door. "Tell Miguel, please, that I would like to go over to the doctor's."

"Oh, *sí*, señor," Dolores said. "He will be glad to hear it."

The household understood that Miguel was enamored of one of Linda's maids. That meant that Miguel would go into a frenzy of squirting himself with scent, with changing his clothes, with oiling his hair.

Keel would brush his teeth.

On the way back to his bedroom, Keel looked in at Linda's old room with its pale blue walls and carpeting. Carpeting was impractical and rare in La Isla; expensive, too. But Linda didn't like her feet to touch tile floors. Even as a tiny girl she had hated the sensation. She now had a house as big as this one herself, all carpeted except for her husband's library, and she had plenty of servants, too. But she had left her amah with Keel. When Linda's first daughter was born, Keel had assumed she would take her old amah, but she had refused. It turned out that Linda had never liked the woman. So Keel was stuck with the heartbroken old lady, who just moped around and depressed everyone in the household.

Thomasino's room next door was lined with his model airplanes and the trophies he had won in the horseshows at the club. Tom was almost thirty, and he was still going to college in the States. He was at Texas Tech in Lubbock now, a senior he insisted. He drove a silver Porsche. Keel discouraged Tom's visits to La Isla. He ran up bills at Keel's club and fucked the maids. Tom wasn't stupid. He just didn't understand that a man didn't fuck his servants.

Keel paused to look into his wife's room. It was much larger than his own and had in it, besides her enormous round bed, a chaise, plus a table with chairs where she had breakfast and sometimes lunch and, if she were having one of her migraines, her tea and then dinner. There were telephones beside the bed, at the chaise and a third one in the bathroom. Keel picked up the phone at the bed and dialed Linda's number. "I thought I'd come say good-bye to you and the girls. I'm flying home early tomorrow. Is this a good time for you? We'll be there as soon as Miguel is ready."

His wife had an enormous marble tub where she liked to lie and soak in bubbles for hours while she talked with friends on the phone and the maids brought her martinis. She started cocktails at four in the afternoon and by the time Keel got home she was wildly, drunkenly animated. It was a relief to have her in the States. When she was at home she insisted on entertaining large groups of her friends two or three times a week. She would play the piano and sing lieder in ugly, guttural German. They would cheer and applaud and drink his gin and eat his food and urge her on and on. Keel was no longer embarrassed by her behavior. Everyone in Puerto Seguro understood. But she was a pain in the ass to have around.

He looked at the huge portrait of her above her outsized bed. She appeared remote, a bit like a young Hedy Lamarr. Keel was amused at the portrait painter's audacity. The young man had shown up suddenly about fifteen years ago and had taken La Isla by storm—mostly because he spoke French. He was in fact from La Grange, Texas, but he knew exactly what his subjects wanted in their portraits, and he delivered it.

Keel's own bedroom could have been a naval officer's quarters. His bed was a foam mattress on a wooden platform. It was not much wider than a cot. Keel had never had a woman in this bed.

Keel climbed into the Buick and as soon as he leaned back in the seat he felt fatigue. He was almost an old man, wasn't he? He let himself sink into the tiredness, trying to see if there was any joy in just accepting the fact that he was sixty-three years old. It was incredible, the swiftness with which he had moved from forty into the sixties. But he was confident that he had at least ten more years of being Keel, the same Keel he had always been. The ulcers hadn't flared up in twenty years now. He kept his weight down. The drinking and the smoking were both under control. His sex . . . he had slowed down, perhaps. But the old slippery dick still responded splendidly when confronted with the right sort of young slit. He touched his crotch and smiled to himself.

Miguel came running, stuffing in the tail of his shiny silver shirt with red roses and black guitars printed all over. It was understood on these occasions that Miguel was not expected to wear his uniform. The doctor's household was part of the family. Miguel said, "I'm sorry, señor, but I got so much sweat unloading those big boxes that my odors would cause a shy young girl to go crazy. I had to shower as soon as I heard we were going to the doctor's house. . . ."

"It's nothing, Miguel, but I can't stay long tonight. I'll just put the little girls to bed."

"Sí. . . ." Miguel backed out of the driveway and waved to the patrolman on the corner. The man had a rifle hanging from the crook in his arm. He nodded.

The doctor's house was less than a five-minute walk from Keel's, and despite the oppressive heat Keel would have enjoyed the exercise. But it simply wasn't safe to walk in the Garden, as this section of the city was called. The Garden was where La Isla's rich lived. It was a walled suburb. Occasionally at night a car with hill people in it would crash past the armed gatekeepers into the neighborhood. Or a group would sneak past a sleeping guard. They would shoot at anyone they found out on the streets and throw a Molotov cocktail at the door of the U.S. trade chief's home and then roar out again.

Miguel drove up into the doctor's drive and stopped at the front door. The girls were waiting for Keel, little faces pressed into the glass panels on either side of the door.

One of the amahs opened the heavy door and the girls rushed squealing. "Papá grande! Papá grande!" He picked up one in each arm. They hugged his neck, each trying to squeeze harder than the other. They were in their nightgowns, one in white and the other in yellow.

"Who are you tonight!" he asked.

"I'm Popeye the Sailor Man!" screamed Olivia.

"I'm Spiderman!" screamed Diane.

"You hug like a spider," Keel said. They were in the front hallway. Linda had covered up the marble floors with rugs. The walls were hung with mirrors in gold frames, antiques from La Isla's colonial period. There was a circular stairway that went up into the ceiling, past a crystal chandelier from Austria. Linda's voice came down from up there. "Hi, Papá. Bring them right on up, will you? It's time they were tucked in."

"No, no!" they screamed. "Story! We want a story!" They were squirming and kicking, and Keel had to hold them tightly as he went up the stairs.

"We'll have a story, girls," he said. "We'll just get you all snug in your beds and then Papá will tell you a story."

Linda was at the top of the stairs, and Keel was surprised again to see what a beautiful woman she was. He usually thought of her as about the age of her daughters, three or four perhaps, running breathlessly through the house. Her dark hair now was pulled back into a bun, but some of it escaped at the front to provide soft curls around her face. Keel remembered that his Aunt Liz's hair had been like that. His mother's, too, until she finally cut it short, claiming that she couldn't handle the waist-long tresses anymore.

"Don't ever cut your hair, Linda," he said.

She laughed and kissed him on the cheek. "Get those little people into their beds and then come down and have a drink with me, will you?"

"Story! Story!"

Keel said, "I have to tell them a story first."

Linda said, "Do *not* tell them about your Great-Aunt Betty and the Indians, Papá. Please? Diane had nightmares."

Diane said, "I love scary stories when Papá grande tells us!"

Olivia said, "I never get scared!"

Keel bent to let the girls down onto the carpeted hall. "Run get in bed and I'll be right there."

"I love you, Papá," Diane yelled.

"I love you more than Diane does, Papá, because I'm older!" Olivia said.

Keel laughed, and Linda said, "Get into bed, girls, and calm down a bit." They disappeared down the hall. "Honestly, Papá . . . You inspire such hysteria in females. I've never understood it."

Keel said, "You look pale. Where's the doctor tonight?"

"He's up in the hills, or he was earlier. He just called from the hospital. He says he's patching up some men who were ambushed in a Jeep this afternoon."

"He thinks he can go anywhere, doesn't he?"

"Everyone seems to know him. I used-to worry like crazy, but this god-awful revolution has been going on now ever since I can remember. . . ."

Olivia was screaming, "We're ready, Papá grande!"

Linda patted his cheek. "All your women are crazy for you. I'll be in the library."

Keel went down the long hallway into the girls' room. He looked in and laughed. Each granddaughter was in her bed, rigid, centered absolutely with covers pulled up to chin. Keel switched off the overhead lights at the door to leave on only the soft lamp on the table between their beds.

"Sit on my bed," Diane said.

"No, no! Sit on my bed. Mine's the softest," Olivia insisted.

"I'll sit on Diane's bed tonight and hold Olivia's hand. All right?"

Diane burst into tears. "Hold my hand, too!"

Keel said, "Okay! It's all right, Diane. I have two hands."

Her tears vanished instantly. Olivia said, "Tell us about how your grandfather threw the mattress over Aunt Betty so the Indians didn't find her."

Diane said, "Mother said he mustn't tell that!"

Keel made his voice as soothing as possible. "Let's just talk tonight. . . ."

Diane said, "Tell us about when you were a little boy. . . ."

Keel wished that he could tell stories the way his mother did. "Well, when I was a little boy I lived on a ranch in the middle of Texas. And my mother had another baby and he was named Field, and then my mother had another baby and he was named Banyan, and then my mother had another baby and he was named Flannel . . ."

Olivia giggled. "Your brothers all have funny names. Why do they have such funny names?"

Keel said, "My father was named Thomas, and he thought that

33

was too ordinary a name, and so he and mother named us for relatives, but they used the last names. Where was I?"

Diane said, "You stopped at Flannel."

"Yes. And a few years after Flannel was born, mother had another baby boy and they named him Horner."

Olivia laughed. "Little Jack Horner sat in the corner—"

Keel said, "I'm going to fly to Texas early in the morning, and I'll get to see all those brothers. They're all old men now, just like me."

"Which war were you in, Papá grande?"

"World War Two."

"That's when you met Gloria and fell in love, wasn't it?"

Keel said, "Yes, that's when I met your grandmother."

Olivia said, "Gloria doesn't look like a grandmother at all."

"Do you think I look like a grandfather?"

"You look like *my* grandfather," Olivia said.

Diane was asleep.

Keel spoke softly. "Do you like school, Livia?"

"It's okay, Papá . . . but some of the kids speak Spanish all the time and the teacher gets mad. I like to draw pictures, and I like to sing when we have music. Diane's already asleep?"

"She's asleep, and now it's time for you to sleep, too."

"Now you can tell *me* about the mean man in Uncle Mac's wagonyard. It's too scary for Diane, and then tell me about the time your mother came home from New York with the new baby brother. . . ."

Keel laughed. "Not tonight, Liv. Maybe I'll have some new stories for you after I visit my mother. You know all my old stories better than I do."

"I wish Mother would go to New York and come back with a baby brother for me. . . ." Olivia snuggled down. "Night, Papá."

Keel stood. "Night, Liv. . . ."

She, too, was asleep.

Linda was lying on the big leather couch with her feet up on the armrest. There were glasses and a bottle on a silver tray on the doctor's ornate desk. The walls of the room were lined with books bound in dark red and green and brown leathers. A glass-covered antique map of La Isla filled one wall.

Keel said, "The air conditioning in the girls' room seems too cold to me. Can I pour you one?"

Linda said, "I'll look in on them when I go up. They sleep better if it's cool, and so do I. I can't stand the humidity. Here it is March, and it's already hot and muggy. I'll have a sniff to keep you company, Papá. Just a thimbleful."

It was very fine brandy. Keel put a small amount in one of the big glasses and handed it to her. She put it on the floor beside her. The crystal base of her glass rang against the red tile floor. Linda said, "He won't let me put a rug in here."

Keel sat in the doctor's chair and concentrated for a moment on the brandy. He let the fumes fill his nose before he sucked a little liquid into his mouth so it could warm his tongue, flooding his senses. He thought of Milagro.

She said, "You look tired. I hate to think of you over there in that big house all by yourself."

Keel laughed. "The place is running over with servants, and you know it. I was thinking about it at dinner tonight. I'm never alone. Would you ask the doctor if he could take two or three of our maids on at the hospital? They just get in each other's way. There are terrible scenes, Dolores says. She's getting fed up. They don't have enough to do."

"When Gloria comes back you'll need them."

"I think maybe she's settled in San Antonio for good. She has her friends there—the old retired army people. Gloria feels at home there. They were all stationed out here once. They know her."

"But she grew up here, Papa. I've spent more time in the States than Gloria has."

"I'll see her day after tomorrow probably. Mama has set up this reunion in Austin so I'm flying there first. . . ."

"Are you and Gloria separated?"

Keel smiled. "Your mother and I have been married, in our own fashion, for thirty-five years. We're still married."

"I hear you have a new girl, Papá."

35

"Jesus! Where do you hear things like that?" Keel was annoyed and he let it show in his voice.

Linda laughed. "Don't get mad at Miguel this time. My friend Tish was going into Sears this morning, and she saw you pick up a country girl right off the street."

"I was just giving her a ride downtown. . . ."

"Do you know that you're a legend in La Isla, Papá? They talk about you up in the hills. When a girl up there gets pregnant she knows that she can—one, get married to the guy, or—two, kill herself, or—three, come down to Puerto Seguro and stand on the corner at the market and wait until the Señor Blanco in the big black car picks her up. Are you going to get this one an abortion?"

Keel said, "This kind of talk makes me uncomfortable. You're beginning to sound like your mother."

Linda said, "I need your help, Papá. I don't understand men at all. The doctor has a new girlfriend, and I want both of them dead."

Keel said, "Don't say that. The doctor is good to you. He's a good husband."

"He sleeps with the nurses at the hospital. I know he does. Tell me why men have to have all these women. Why do you have to have all your girls? When will you slow down? My God, Papá, you're past sixty! Is it just because Gloria has always been such a phony? I know she would tax a saint with her silly chatter and her drinking."

Keel took another sip of brandy and waited a little. "There is no evil in it, Linda. Women . . . wives think it happens because of some failure on their part, but some of us just need to . . . I can't explain it to you. I never could explain it to your mother. She was hurt at first, and I promised. . . . I meant it, too. Every time I meant it. But I like women. New women. When I'm with a new woman I never know whether or not she will—I guess I think I'm still young . . . that I'm not going to die. I don't have to think about dying." Was that the truth of it? Keel wondered.

Linda asked softly, "Are you so afraid of dying?"

"Of course. I hate getting old. . . ."

"But that's what's so amazing about you, Papá! You know that! You look ten years younger than any other man your age. It's all right for a man to get old. You still attract young women. . . ."

"I can still be useful to them, and so they put up with certain frailties, the sagging flesh. Look at my hands. They are beginning to look like my father's hands before he had his stroke. They are white, and the veins stick out . . . brown spots. The skin flakes. Ugh . . ."

"Where is Grandpa's ring?"

"I don't wear it anymore. I'll give it to you if you want to have it cut down. I never really got along very well with him. Did you know that? He never approved of me. Everyone thought he was a saint. Mother insisted that I have his ring because I am the oldest. It wasn't just the girls and the drinking and my cigars, either. He was a most unworldly man. . . . He thought I was too sharp in business deals."

"Fathers and sons! You're just feeling sorry for yourself. Grandpa was proud of you, and you know it. He loved to brag about your rich wife and your swimming pool and your twenty servants."

Keel put down his empty glass and stood up. "I've got to go, honey."

Linda said, "Thank you for coming over to see the girls. They adore you."

Keel nodded. "Sometimes Olivia holds her mouth in a way that makes me think of my mother. I must have some new photos of them when I go home. Do you have any new ones?"

"Of course. The doctor takes pictures all the time. I'll give you an envelope full for Grandmama. I guess I'm pregnant again, Papá."

"Well, that's wonderful, isn't it?"

"If it's a boy this time the doctor says we don't have to have any more."

"Is that all right with his church?"

"You know the doctor is far more important than any church." There was scorn in her voice.

Keel said, "Take care of yourself."

"Of course. I'll tell Tina to send Miguel out to the car." She brought him an envelope with photos in it, and he put it in his pocket.

"Give Grandmama my love." She kissed him on the cheek. "Have a good trip. You'll be back Sunday week?"

"Sooner, maybe, if I can get some new money quickly. I may fly up to Washington for a day, too, as long as I'm in the States."

Keel let himself out the front door in the flood of the outdoor lights and squinted to check his watch. It was almost ten. It seemed much later.

The sounds of the shots were loud, echoing in a distant part of the house. Keel sat up. He turned on the light beside his bed and moved deliberately. There were shouts and the noise of car tires screaming. Keel pulled on his pants and slipped his feet into thonged slippers. His toes were crooked, ugly, an old man's pale feet.

A truck roared away. Keel went down the hall and unbolted the door that separated the bedroom wing from the rest of the house.

The women were in the main hallway, holding onto each other, wailing, waiting for him. He switched on the lights in the back patio and said, "Tell them to shut up, Dolores."

He went out, across the bricks, inhaling the damp tropic night, aware of the air's heaviness after the crisp air conditioning inside. He opened the garage door. The lights were on.

Miguel was sprawled on the floor with blood seeping out from under him. The Buick had been pushed back onto the driveway so that someone could get at the crates. They were gone.

The women who had followed him saw Miguel and screamed.

"Shut up," he said. Dolores was there, her old eyes wide with fright. He said to her, "Go telephone the doctor and then call the police."

Where was that goddamned patrol? Keel was paying a hundred pesetas a week to the neighborhood association for protection, and the stupid guards were never around when something happened.

Part of Keel's mind was working out a scenario. He was certain now that he had been used, that he should have known from the beginning that something like this could happen. Why hadn't he hidden the crates, or put them in some safe place, locked up? It might not have made any difference. If the hill people wanted his guns, they would get them. But he didn't like being used. It was too dangerous. Thirty years of doing business in La Isla could go down the drain in an instant if Alberto thought he was helping the hill people. His ass would be booted out—or worse.

Miguel moaned. Keel knelt beside him. The silver shirt was stained with darker red among the flowers. Miguel must have been sleeping in his shirt when he heard them moving the boxes out of the garage. Keel went quickly to the back door of the house and shouted into the kitchen: "Did you call the doctor, Dolores? Call the hospital now and have them send an ambulance!"

Dolores said, "*Madre Dios!* Miguel still lives?"

"Yes, yes. . . . Go telephone."

Cars were arriving now, screeching to a halt. By the time Keel got back to the garage it was overrun with uniformed men milling around. "Don't touch him," Keel said to a couple of patrolmen who were kneeling over Miguel. "He made a sound. I've sent for the doctor." An officer, ignoring Keel, repeated to the men, "Don't touch him! A doctor is coming."

The doctor had to leave his car out on the street. He nodded gravely to Keel, knelt beside Miguel and, when the ambulance came, supervised loading Miguel onto the stretcher.

Keel invited the officer to come into the house. On the way past the kitchen he asked Dolores to bring them some coffee. It was 2:30 A.M.

The captain's name was Mero. He seemed to have been intimidated by the doctor. Of course he knew Keel, but foreigners were to be treated with a certain contempt, no matter how big their homes or how many cars and servants they had. Keel was not at all sure whether or not he had ever seen the young officer before. Mero had the standard, carefully trimmed mustache of the La Isla official.

They sat in Keel's study, which was just off the living room. There were no books, just an old yellow oak table from the States and a couple of worn leather chairs. Keel offered the captain a cigar. The captain bit off the end and let Keel hold a lighter for him. His boots were beautifully polished. "I gather from my questioning of your servants, Señor Bonner, that you have been robbed?"

Keel nodded. "Three boxes . . . wooden crates, really. They had just arrived today. If you will excuse me for a moment, Captain, I believe I brought the papers home with me in my jacket. . . ." He had started to say that the crates had held sewing machines, but then he remembered García's documents. In his dressing room Keel found the jacket he had worn and removed the papers. He hadn't bothered to read them earlier. He stood in the closet doorway trying to read what García had written on the forms. The man's writing was impossible. But certainly there was no mention of guns or rifles or automatic weapons of any kind.

Keel took the papers back to the study and presented them to the captain. Mero studied them, frowning. Apparently he couldn't read García's scribbles either. He looked up. "Señor?" He was asking for an explanation.

Keel could stall a few seconds more as Dolores brought in the coffee. Keel noted that she was using an enameled pot from the kitchen and the brown native cups and saucers instead of Gloria's fine china. The captain did not rate very high with Dolores.

Keel said, "I had just had the three boxes unloaded in the garage tonight. I bought them at auction today from the customs office. I was told that they contained objects seized from a boat in the harbor. I did not open them so I cannot say for certain what the crates contained."

"You mean you bought them without knowing what was in them?"

Keel nodded gravely. Better to look stupid than say something dangerous. "That is the way I often do business here, Captain. I got the crates for three hundred pesetas—isn't that what the papers say?" The captain checked and nodded. "Your customs office is not usually in the business of buying and selling goods. I am. You will find when you ask at the customs office that we have done business in this manner before."

"You must have some idea about what the crates contained. One of your servants said they were heavy. You wouldn't buy rocks for all those pesetas."

Keel looked at his watch. "I think the boxes might have contained small machines—sewing machines, kitchen mixers, appliances. There are no laws in La Isla to prevent a businessman from importing and selling such items because they are not manufactured here."

"Yes . . . but they are very expensive," the captain said.

Keel nodded. "That's why I can afford to bid on such shipments."

The captain twisted the cigar slowly in his lips, sucking it softly. After a time, he said, "What if the crates had guns in them? . . . Do you think such a thing is possible?"

Keel looked directly at him. "It's impossible. Your customs people would never sell guns to anyone on La Isla. And I am a friend of the president and his gracious wife. I certainly would never bring any guns into their country. Do you think for one minute that I would have anything to do with the Communists? With your hill people? You know how Americans feel about Communism."

Mero said, "I'm not sure I understand you Americans. Business is everything with you, isn't it?"

"Ah, but one has no business without the blessing of the president. Isn't that so?"

"I have heard it said." The captain looked away. "But I must go." He stood. "I shall take your documents, if I may?"

Keel nodded. "I hope that you will find the men who shot my driver."

"Good night, Señor Bonner."

"Captain . . ." Dolores was waiting in the hallway. She showed the officer out the back way.

Back in bed, Keel wondered if he would have to mention anything about any of this in his report. Did he look dumb? There was something uncomfortable about being used this way by

41

everyone. The Navy expected him to provide it with a continuing flow of information. He had been its chief source of intelligence from La Isla ever since he arrived just after the war. Its financing had put him in business. It probably was one of the longest such arrangements the Navy had.

And the Navy, the United States, wanted Alberto in power. The United States could keep its bases on La Isla as long as Alberto was in the palace. The United States didn't want another Cuba, and now Keel realized that inadvertently he had been helping the revolutionaries. . . . He would have to delay his flight tomorrow until he was certain there weren't going to be serious repercussions. García was the key.

Ah, then there was Milagro. How nice that she had come along. . . . She was safe at the hotel. He would now have time to see her again early tomorrow. . . . No one else could screw her even while he was away. León, the manager, was well paid to look after the girls. León did not like country girls at all, Keel was certain. He was too fastidious. León probably preferred the hotel's bellboys. . . .

Keel stepped out of the elevator at the Nacional the next morning after a visit upstairs. Milagro liked junk jewelry. He had given her some earrings that Gloria would never miss. Probably Milagro was pregnant, as Linda had guessed. He would have to see that she had an abortion. Linda was right about his reputation. Milagro had been waiting for him on the sidewalk. When country girls got into trouble . . . He shrugged.

García was moving toward him in the lobby. "Well, Señor Bonner, this certainly is a surprise. May I walk out with you?"

Keel was certain that García had been waiting for him. He smiled and nodded and shook his hand. "Would you like to have a cup of coffee with me?"

García said, "What a kind invitation! But I must get back to my office. . . ."

They went out of the hotel entrance together, into the blinding afternoon light. García fell into step beside him. García turned his face into a tragic mask. It was a sudden, almost comic transformation. "I understand that you had a robbery at your house last night?"

Keel nodded. "I have had to delay a business trip."

García continued: "Those of us who live in the city always imagine that you in the Garden are safe from such terrible problems. You have your own police, have you not?"

"I guess they can't be everyplace at once. The crates were stolen, and my driver was shot."

"Ah. Will he live?"

"The doctor believes so. There was a lot of blood lost."

García pulled his hand from his pocket and stuck it out as if to shake Keel's hand. "Well, it was good to run into you this morning," he said abruptly. "I am truly sorry about your misfortune, but there is no reason now for you to delay your trip. The police understand how these things happen, don't you think? ¡Adiós!" While he was talking he transferred a roll of money into the palm of Keel's hand. Keel put it into his pocket and strolled across the street to his office.

Once inside, he hung up his jacket, removed the roll that García had slipped to him and dropped it onto his desk. He smoothed the bills out and counted quickly, smiling to himself. García had been true to his word. Their deal had been very profitable for Keel. The money had been doubled in twenty-four hours. Poor Miguel was hardly a plus, however.

But more important, Keel realized that he had acquired a piece of exceedingly valuable information: García, a keyman in the customs office, was helping to supply guns to the hill people. And García was able to handle the police, too. It was all very, very interesting.

That information offered all sorts of possibilities for a profitable future. Keel saw no reason why he couldn't start putting it to use by reducing the squeeze that customs always put on him. He would tell García that Miguel's hospital expenses were heavy. García would understand.

The best thing about learning to drink gin without ice was that he could celebrate at almost any time or place. There was a bottle of Holland gin in his desk. He would add a dash of bitters. . . .

His secretary in the outer office heard the click of bottle on glass. "Are you all right, señor?" she called out.

"See if you can get me on an afternoon flight to the States now, will you, Nita? Mother is going to be upset because I'm running late. . . ."

"Then everything is all right?"

He sipped the warm pink liquid. "*Sí, querida mia.* Never better."

TWO

Field Bonner

FIELD'S mother started talking the moment he came in her kitchen door. He smiled and grunted. He always spoke so softly that few people could understand him, and his mother's hearing was failing. The good thing about Field was that, unlike her other sons and friends, he never said anything loud enough so that he upset her. If she looked flustered by something he said, he would try the opposite. This morning their talk went something like this:

He mumbled, "How's your sore hip this morning, Mama?"

"What, honey?"

He grinned.

She laughed. "I was just waiting for you. . . ."

So they got along fine, which was a tribute to Field's patience and understanding.

There were roosters all over her kitchen—on towels, on a paper napkin holder, salt and pepper shakers—all gifts from her daughters-in-law, from friends, from her sisters in Fort Worth. They all thought she liked roosters. In fact, Field knew his mother had never liked the nasty male things, strutting around the backyard, jumping up on the poor hens whenever they felt like it. Disgusting.

Field drank his coffee black. His mother liked to wait on him. He unwrapped a cigar and put it in his mouth, but he didn't light it. His mother detested smoking.

47

She limped back from the cabinet to the kitchen table. The window looked out on a two-foot-tall, dancing-girl statue in a white birdbath. His mother said, "The smell of wet cigars always makes me think of your father's papa. He was a sweet old man, but he did have his nasty habits."

Field said, "He and I used to play dominoes even after he was blind."

"What, son?"

"Dominoes."

"Oh, yes. He was a fine domino player, but he couldn't stand to have a woman beat him. He'd rather play with you little boys. . . ." She went into a long story about how Grandpa Bonner once accused her of cheating during a domino game.

Field had heard it before, many times. Two or three mornings a week, Field stopped by his mother's house to have a cup of coffee with her. He would, at her insistence, listen to the knocking noises in her heater. He would take her garbage out. If she had some problem with an appliance, he would tell her he'd send out a repairman. His father had always done all these things. She was spoiled, Field thought, but it was too late to change her.

He listened through the story, smiling in the right places, finished his coffee and stood. "Uh-huh," he grunted.

"Thanks for stopping by. Is Carolyn all right?"

"Uh-huh. . . ."

"Oh, I've been so excited about it, and then I almost forgot to ask you. What time do you think Flannel will show up tonight?"

"When did he say he was leaving?"

"He was getting on his plane this morning, but then he has to get here from Dallas."

Field said, "I imagine he'll be here sometime after supper, if that's what you're wondering about." He got up and went out through the garage. His mother followed him, teetering slightly without her cane. He paused beside his car to light his cigar.

At 7:30 A.M. the sun was well up in the sky, the air clear. Field played golf every day, unless it was pouring rain. His mother said, "Have a nice game this afternoon. Oh, I know what it was I've been wanting to tell you! I was joking on the telephone with

Banyan, and I said that you'd be at his recital if you didn't have a golf game, and you know what Banyan said about your golf playing? He said that he thinks you're some kind of throwback to the Bonners who came to Texas before the War Between the States. You have to keep proving something, he said. Banyan says your golf games are like some kind of Old West shoot-out. It's a way of proving that you're better than the other old men in town." She laughed and clapped her hands in delight.

Field grinned at her. "Banyan thinks too much," he said.

Field had a splendid chair at his desk. It was old and ugly, but it swiveled and the leather was smooth. It fit his bottom exactly right. If the office was empty and quiet, he might fall into a kind of stupor during which he never moved at all. Customers coming in the front to buy stationery supplies or leave a classified ad would accuse him of being asleep. But he wasn't. Often his mind raced through a dozen concerns, immediate and past, during these periods. But it was also a kind of meditation. Sometimes after such a spell he would feel a surge of energy.

Carolyn had long ago learned to recognize Field's withdrawal. She would say cheerily, "Oh, lookee, Field is having one of his fits." This morning, however, Carolyn hadn't yet come in, and Mynalou had gone across the square on some errand. In the quiet of the empty building, Field, who had been writing an editorial about the need to get the weeds mowed out in Lady Park, slipped into one of his spells. The park triggered memories of playing when he was little. Then, perhaps because his mother had mentioned Banyan this morning, Field remembered the time Banyan had gone into the hospital as a six-year-old to be circumcised. Field and Keel were coming down the hall with some little metal cars they had bought for Banyan at the five-and-dime when they heard Banyan's drugged voice crying out, "Oh! My little do-no-which-it hurts!" The nurses were giggling in the halls. Field had been painfully embarrassed. Dr. Hansen had checked Field's penis, but, fortunately for Field, the foreskin slipped back easily, and he had been spared Banyan's ordeal. Field scratched his crotch. He was the only one of the five who was still all in one

49

piece, as nature intended. It was a source of some satisfaction to him.

The hospital today was the same aging box of yellow stucco, owned by the doctors who practiced there—Hansen, Daniels and Doc Allen. There was no problem with credit. Either bank in Lady would lend the doctors any amount they needed to expand. The doctors had the highest incomes in town, Field was certain, except for old man Clark, maybe, and the Roaks family.

Field tried to pull his mind back to his typewriter, to force himself to get down on paper a few words about Lady Park.

The doctors were stalling. They had been stalling for months, even years. Why?

Carolyn sailed in and gave Field a pat on the cheek. "Good morning," she said.

Field nodded absently.

Carolyn said, "Oh, were you thinking about your column? I'm sorry I broke in."

"Uh-huh," Field grunted, looking at her now, seeing her skinny and nervous but pretty, fresh, with her lipstick on perfectly, her hair silvered, frozen in place by spray. She had just come from Lulu's Beauty Salon.

"You can go have your coffee now, honey. I saw Buddy on his way to the drugstore. You might hint to him that he ought to pay us something on what he owes."

Field said, "I guess I'll go over to the courthouse first. Maybe I'll go for coffee afterward. Tell Mynalou I'll help with the classifieds this afternoon if she needs it."

Carolyn laughed. "Right. That'll scare her into getting them all done. She doesn't think you're careful enough."

Field was at the door, fingering the open-closed sign. "Someday I'll show you two women and put out this whole newspaper by myself."

The courthouse was an ugly stone castle in the middle of the square. Field nodded to the old man climbing up onto the high sidewalk and to a mother and baby who were headed for the five-and-dime. It was always the busiest store on Field's side of the square.

On the courthouse lawn was a big concrete monument, a seven-foot slab in the shape of the State of Texas, mounted on a four-foot-square box of poured concrete. On the base was printed in an imitation of chiseled lettering: LADY, TEXAS, SEAT OF COOPER COUNTY, ESTABLISHED 1842. Up on the map part, where Lady was located, there was a glass star, lighted at night by a bulb inside. At Christmastime, Juan Hernandez, the courthouse janitor, put in a red bulb. The monument had been erected to mark the centennial of the town, just a few weeks before Pearl Harbor. Thomas Bonner had admired it greatly, but Field thought it was the worst eyesore in a town full of old, weather-beaten eyesores. He once considered mounting a newspaper campaign to get the monument removed, but his mother, who claimed she, too, thought it was ugly as sin, said that Field could just tear the town apart. What she meant was, I hate it, but your father thinks it's wonderful, so don't make us choose sides on this thing. By the time Thomas died, Field had grown accustomed to the monument, and he knew that he, too, would miss it if anything happened to it.

As a matter of fact, he wrote one of his most-praised editorials after some kids spray-painted a pumpkin face on the concrete map—the star was the nose and the mouth crossed just about where Uvalde is located—one Halloween. The surface had to be sandblasted clean. "To deface the great State of Texas is bad enough," Field had written, "but to mar a monument that has come to represent the solid, stable and enduring values of this community is a particularly dark and perverse crime. . . ." Only his mother suspected that he was having fun.

Right after that, Field was playing golf one day with Emmett Todd. Todd worked at the Lady State Bank. He was two strokes ahead, going into the eighth hole, when Field asked him in a quiet voice, "Did your boys paint that pumpkin face on the Texas map?"

Emmett looked down at the toes of his boots and flushed. "Goddamnit, Field, why do you even say a thing like that! You know my boys never in the world would do a thing like that! Why, their granddaddy helped to put that big thing up in place back in 1942."

51

After that, however, Emmett's game just fell apart. Field won two dollars off him.

When he was a child, the family always came to town on Saturdays, and Field would play around and inside the courthouse. His father would go to the feed store. His mother would load up a cart at the Piggly Wiggly and then shop at J.C. Penney. "These remnants of yours have gotten high as a cat's back, Miss Dolly," she said to the clerk at Penney's. "Why at ten cents a yard for little old flimsy cotton scraps, a woman would do better just using a cotton flannel blanket instead of going to all the work it takes to make a quilt."

"It wouldn't be as pretty as one of your quilts, Mrs. Bonner."

"I especially wanted a good red. Mr. Bonner loves anything that's red."

Miss Dolly said, "The new Baptist preacher's wife loves red, too. Wouldn't you know it? She comes in here on Fridays when we first put the ends out, and she'll buy every red on the table. Solids and prints both."

Field was almost five years old. He was in an anguish of boredom, jumping from foot to foot. His mother said, "Oh, all right. Go on over to the courthouse and play, honey. Papa will honk when we're ready to go. Tell Keel we're going home about four if you see him. You listen for the horn, now."

Field darted out.

"Watch out for the cars, Field!" his mother sang after him.

There was a lot of traffic around the square on Saturdays, a whole herd of honking pickup trucks in from the country.

Field found a couple of other boys about his age, and they roamed the cool halls of the courthouse, peeked into the open offices—empty of clerks on Saturdays—hid in the shrubs outside, climbed the pecan trees at either end of the great lawn, watched the girls turn cartwheels. "Why can girls do cartwheels and boys can't?"

Once, intrigued by her quickness, Field squatted down on the sidewalk and played jacks with a girl. Her rubber ball had a red surface that was crazed like an old china plate. She showed Field how to start by picking up the little metal stars one at a time, then two at a time, three, and eventually all ten in one grand sweep. She began to do Shooting Stars and Around the World and other elaborate variations. She was wonderfully skillful.

When Field got home he found a rubber ball that had once been attached to a rubber band on a wooden paddle, and he went out to gather ten little stones about the size of jacks. He squatted down on the porch and began to play. The stones were harder to pick up than the pointed metal jacks, but gradually he could do it.

Keel spotted him. "Uh-uh, Field! That's a girl's game. That's just like jumping rope. Don't you know what girls' games will do to you? Every time you play a girls' game your do-no-which-it gets smaller until if you keep on doing it, it goes into reverse up inside your body and you have to sit down to pee just like a girl."

Field threw the ball at Keel, missed and then jumped up and began pounding on him.

Keel laughed at the fury he had provoked.

Their mother in the kitchen heard the fighting. "Play pretty, boys," she sang out. She was cutting up peaches for preserves. The kitchen was hot and steaming from her kettles of boiling fruit and jars.

Flannel, who had just begun to walk, stood at the screen door, crying to get out.

Field pulled out the volume of records on land title transfers. It was gray, heavy, with stiff, cream-colored pages. He wasn't sure what he was looking for, or when the transfer might have taken place. But it was in going through these records that he had first stumbled onto the veterans' land scandal that had set off a state-wide investigation. The stories ended with B. B. Holingsworth going to the state prison in Huntsville. B.B. had been one of Thomas's oldest friends in Lady, so it was a disappointment to Thomas when it turned out that B.B. had swindled all those Mexican veterans out of land they had bought with low-interest loans guaranteed by the state. B.B. spent a lot of his ill-gotten gain on his lawyers during his trial, and he came home from Huntsville an old man. But he was rich again in no time at all. Some men just know how to make money. Money seems to follow them as if they were magnets, was the way Field's mother explained it.

Field flipped through the ledger backward, rapidly, guided only by the vague feeling that he would spot anything odd if he happened upon it.

And, sure enough, less than two months back into the records, he spotted Doc's name. Doc Allen had taken title to the old Codder place out on the south side of Lady, about a mile below Whiteland Hill. Now, how had such a deal happened so quietly? Field hadn't heard a word about it. Mrs. Codder had died, and Field now remembered that there had been some talk about her will, but the minute she was in the ground and Field had printed her obit, she had been forgotten. Field closed the big, gray land-title volume and went for the ledgers where wills were recorded.

The document was there, filed neatly just as it was supposed to be. The remarkable thing was that nobody apparently had noticed it when it was probated, because nobody in town had commented on it. Maybe it was because Mrs. Codder's place was so small. Field was surprised to see that she had only two hundred and thirty acres left at the time she died. She had been selling off pieces of her land for twenty years. And it was poor stuff, too, mostly white clay that nothing would grow in except mesquite and prickly pear. She had left the last of it to Doc. But her property was not far from the end of Lady that still was growing, and the town easily could go out that far one day. When it did, Doc would have himself a very valuable piece of real estate. It could make a rich man richer. Especially since he got it for nothing.

Field sang out to the woman behind the counter in the front office. "I put them all back, Lois Ann."

"In the right slots? You don't look carefully sometimes when you are finishing up, Field."

"Oh, you got me cured. I don't want you yelling at me."

She had been one of Keel's classmates all through school, one of the many who had loved Keel. So she always asked, "What do you hear from Keel?"

"He's coming up from La Isla this weekend. To Austin, and then I guess he'll come visit Mama."

"Who would ever have thought that boy would go way down there and just never come back? . . . I wish he'd stop off and see me the next time he's visiting your mother."

"I'll tell him, Lois Ann."

She giggled. "You do that."

The Lady Drugstore was on the northeast corner of the square. It was owned by the doctors at the hospital and presided over by Milton Perry, a man the doctors had plucked from a Lady High School graduating class and sent on to the University of Texas to become a pharmacist. Milton dutifully returned and took over Lady Drug just as the doctors had planned.

The man behind the counter was Eli Nowkes, now in his seventies. Eli had been at Lady Drug as long as anyone could remember. He had started there as a child sweeping out. He was now legally blind, but he still drove his car. His glasses were thick, with a smaller round lens set in the middle of the glass. It gave him a wise look that was misleading. He always wore a tie and an apron. "Here's Field, come in for his daily banana split," Eli muttered in greeting. It was a joke that went back to Field's childhood when Lady Drug offered such delicacies at its splendid, marble-topped soda-fountain counter. But it was Keel, as a nine-year-old, who had once come into the drugstore, ordered a banana split, tasted it and then announced to Eli, "I believe I could eat a banana split every day of my life." Keel had started young developing a taste for things tropical.

Lady Drug had long since given up keeping bananas around on the rare chance that someone might like to buy a split. Nowadays Eli had Coke, soda water, a few flavorings, three kinds of ice cream, coffee and, twice a week, doughnuts off a truck from a Brownwood bakery. The coffee was watery, pale and scorched tasting. It sat in a Pyrex pot on a hot plate behind the counter from seven in the morning until it was all drunk, at which time Eli would make another pot for the midafternoon regulars.

Field preferred Eli's coffee after it had been sitting for a few hours because the prolonged heating helped it develop some character.

"Hey, Milt, come sit with me a minute, and I'll buy you a coffee this morning," Field called out to the back.

Eli said, "Milt won't drink my coffee, and you know it."

"That's because he's smart. He knows it rots out the innards, Eli, and makes your earlobes swell up."

Eli grinned. "You are trying to pull my leg, Field. Lumber Forrest was in here last week, and he claimed my coffee was causing hair to grow on the end of his dick. I told him if he wasn't so stingy with his pecker such a thing never would happen, and it wasn't right for him to go around blaming my coffee for his hairy tool."

Eli put the coffee in front of him. Field inspected it and then handed the saucer back. "Your saucer's got a big chip out of it. Give me a whole one, will you?"

"Good Godalmighty, Field! Who would ever see a little old chip like that but you! I feel sorry for what Carolyn has to put up with. You are one persnickety boy."

Field chuckled. "You make me feel good, Eli. I'm going to be sixty any day now, and you still call me a boy."

Eli inspected his saucers from the shelf by holding them up just an inch or two from his glasses until he found a whole one. "It's not like you was going to be drinking out of the saucer . . ."

"My papa taught me not to," Field said.

Eli frowned. "Your papa was a saint, and I do miss him even with him dead nine years now."

Milt came out of the back. He was balding and pink so that he looked much older than his thirty-two years. He wore rimless glasses that sparkled. But there was no humor in him. He supported a houseful of women: his mother, who worked in Lulu's Beauty Salon when she was sober, and his grandmother who was bedridden. Milt's wife had been married before, and she had four daughters by previous husbands. She and Milt also had a little girl of their own. The child needed one more operation to correct a clubfoot.

"Well," Field said, "how are all your ladies?"

"Granny's mean as ever," Milt said. "She wouldn't eat anything this morning because Mama wouldn't buy her some yellow satin so she could make herself a blouse. The old lady can't really see well enough to sew anymore, and she just cuts up perfectly good cloth and then gets all upset when she can't put it together right. So there's a lot of yelling, and that upsets the baby . . ."

Field chuckled, but Milt continued without smiling, reeling off the account of his chaotic homelife.

Eli brought Milt a cup of tea with the bag still in it and then went to the back of the store where he read comic books held up to his face and smoked cigarettes, setting the comics on fire repeatedly. Milt would sniff and call out, "Smoke, Eli."

Field sipped his coffee and was patient. When Milt paused to try his tea, Field said, "Speaking of ladies, Milt, I was wondering if you knew what it was that old lady Codder died of last fall?"

"Why, it was just old age. Everything just wore out in her at about the same time. She was well past ninety. Mama swears she was ninety-eight, if she was a day. You had it all in the paper, how she was the last one of a pioneer Lady family."

"She was one of Doc's patients, wasn't she?"

"My, yes. For years. Doc himself was the one who looked after her."

"I always wondered why when she got so feeble she didn't go into the Golden Arches Nursing Home," Field said.

"Oh, Doc said she wouldn't give up living in her house. It was packed full of cut-glass vases, all kinds of nice dodads and marble-topped tables and rugs from India and China. Towards the end, Doc was going out to see her every day, and he got that Mexican woman in to clean and help look after her."

"So the old lady just wasted away. . . ."

"There must have been a lot of pain. Doc was giving her a lot of medication toward the end."

"What do they give old people these days to make them comfortable?"

"Oh, she went through a half dozen different drugs during her last year or so. The truth is that she had once been a heavy drinker, and Doc was always scared to leave any medicine around out there. That's why she called him so often, and he always went right out and looked after her. He never found out in the early days who was taking her the bourbon, he said, but she was putting down a fifth a day when he first took over her case. . . ."

Field listened, thinking of the wasted old lady, an addict, lying out there in the country, calling for the doctor, for her pain-killing drugs.

Mrs. Abner came in with a prescription, and Milt got up from the counter. She handed him the scrap of paper and said, "How's your mother, Field?"

"Oh, she's fine, Mrs. Abner. She's resting up to play Bolivia tomorrow at Aunt Judy's, I believe."

"She is just the most amazing thing, the way she just goes on living all by herself and doing all those things for the church."

Field smiled and nodded and called out, "I've got to get back, Milt." He put two quarters on the counter.

Milt called out, "See you."

Eli yelled, "Thank you, Field. You all have a nice day now, hear?" It was an imitation of an actor Eli watched on a television comedy about small-town people.

Sometimes Field thought that what he liked best about putting out a newspaper in Lady were the details. As a young reporter in Fort Worth, he had been restless, covering the Tarrant County courthouse. In Lady there were always little things that needed doing: a late piece of copy from his correspondent, Mrs. Ford, over in Rochelle that he could set in type himself after Mynalou had gone home, trimming a photo on the big paper cutter, re-working type on a page to get in a late advertisement. Often it was just busywork. Mynalou was better and faster. He thought he probably got his interest in doing the little things from his mother, who always had crochet or quilt pieces in her hands, working away while she talked, reading a book and watching television—all at the same time.

Mynalou was in the office when Field returned, and, as always, she was very much in charge. Both Field and Carolyn deferred to her. She was much younger, but she was smart and full of energy. She was there when Carolyn's father bought the newspaper to get Field and Carolyn to leave Fort Worth and move back to Lady. Mynalou "knew where all the bodies were buried." That was the way she explained her job. But in addition she wasn't afraid to ask any advertiser in town to pay up. "If he owes us money, Field, he should pay. I don't understand why you pussyfoot around about money so much. This is a business. You can't pay my salary unless Lead Thompson pays for his classifieds. Right? That's how the Lawsons got into such a mess and had to sell out to your daddy-in-law. You let folks run up these hundred-dollar-plus bills, and it just makes it harder for me to collect. I'll stop off on the way home to see him." Mynalou had been married once to a boy from Salt Gap. He didn't produce up to her expectations so she divorced him and he drifted on.

Danny Lorens stuck his head in the door. "Hey, Field, old Madison has turned himself into some kind of an optimist. He's gone and put a big black umbrella in the gun rack of his pickup truck!" He hooted with laughter and slammed the door.

At noon Carolyn and Field went home for lunch. He drove his Lincoln. She followed in her rebuilt Thunderbird convertible. Their house was low, ranch style, on a small lot with similar houses all around it. They had added so many rooms that it was more than double its original size.

Carolyn's bathroom was the most spectacular addition. It was all white marble with a sunken tub. The room was the talk of Lady when they first had it installed. Strangers would knock on the door and ask to come in and see it. Carolyn told everyone she'd never move away and leave her bathroom.

On the way through the kitchen, Field got a bottle of Carta Blanca from the refrigerator and then dropped into his chair opposite a wall-size television screen. He touched the buttons on the arm of his chair and wiggly lines appeared on the screen, flopping over and over and gradually turning into a picture of a man, larger than life, at a desk, reading the noon news. It was on cable, from an Austin station. The man's shirt was pink.

Carolyn said, "Oh, I hate his voice. . . ." She was busy at the counter, putting together a salad, setting out the ingredients for sandwiches. "Do you want iced tea?"

"Uh. . . ."

"Uh, yes or uh, no?"

"Beer." He meant, I already have a beer.

Carolyn put his lunch on a tray and set it on a small table before him. "Is Flannel coming in tonight?"

He nodded.

"I bet your mama is excited, isn't she?" She went into her bedroom and fell onto her bed.

After Field ate he unbuckled his belt and unzipped his fly. His belly sagged out. He lay down. The couch, like the chair in his office, had his shape impressed in the leather cushions. He snuggled down into place.

The low sounds from the television were just a nice hum, comforting. The leather was cool. The couch's odor always made him think of his saddle and the pony he had had when he was ten. It was a nasty Shetland that had tried to bite him every time he wanted to put the bit in its mouth. Field's father always had to threaten the animal with a stick. Its name was Delopholus. It had been named for his mother's voice teacher from San Angelo, a man who wore a toupee. Mr. Delopholus's toupee was the first one ever seen in Lady. That was back in 1928. . . .

Field thought that after a while he would go out to the golf course and see who was there and maybe tonight after supper he and Carolyn could round up a bridge game. . . .

The next morning Field thought he would stop off and see Flannel. Field parked in his mother's driveway. He could see them through her kitchen window. For an instant he thought of his father who had sat in the same place, the same way, a tall, thin man, too. They were having coffee and talking—Field was sure that they had been at it for a couple of hours anyway. He opened the back door and said, "I hope you made a cup for me."

His mother jumped. "Oh, honey! I was hoping you would stop by."

Flannel stood and shook Field's hand. Although Field saw him every year when Flannel came down for his annual visit to their mother, Field was surprised each time at how much older Flannel had become than the teenager who was lodged in Field's memory. Field said, "The rest of us are managing to add a little poundage with the passage of years. What's the matter with you?"

Flannel laughed. "You're going to be all poundage if you don't watch it. What a gut!"

"Son!" their mother said, as if shocked by the word.

Field hated to be reminded of it, but he grinned because he had, after all, asked for it. "Your hair's gone all gray. What are you worrying about these days?" There. That evened the score.

"The oil business is booming, but I've got a show I can't raise the money for—"

Their mother interrupted. "Play producing is like gambling, isn't it? I don't think you ought to be doing it—even as a hobby, Flannel. Can I pour you a cup of coffee, Field?"

"What do you think I stopped by for?"

"You see, Flannel?" their mother said. "He's gotten where he talks sassy to me all the time." She hobbled over to get a cup and saucer and to pour coffee from the pot on the stove. "Sit down with us, Field. Are you and Carolyn all set to drive to Austin after lunch?"

Field hated the delicate little chairs his mother had in her kitchen. They had needlepoint-covered seats, each with a rooster in a different color. The chairs made him feel even more gross. But he pulled one up across the table from Flannel. Their mother sat between them. Field said, "I'm on my way to shoot the new cheerleaders this morning, and then if nothing comes up . . ."

She said, "Now you remember that Banyan is playing at the university at eight. I'm so excited! Won't it be glorious to have all of us there to hear him?"

Field winked at Flannel and said, "Mama, I had to listen to Banyan practice for so many years that I don't care if I never hear him play again."

"Son!" She pretended shock again. "Well, it won't hurt you just this once. You boys ought to be proud of your brother."

Flannel said, "I'm all set, Mama. I'm Banyan's biggest fan, remember?"

Field said, "I don't see why he didn't take up the guitar and write songs and sing like Willie Nelson. He'd be famous and rich by now."

Their mother was indignant. "There is serious, good music, and then there is all that other, Field. I hate to dignify it with the name of music. I don't know why you have to pretend you're just a simple old country boy, Field. You heard plenty of fine music when you were growing up."

"That doesn't mean I liked it," Field said. "I always headed for the pasture on Saturday afternoons." He asked Flannel, "You remember how Mama always had to have on the Texaco opera, Flannel?"

Flannel shrugged. "Mama turned me into a sort of fan, I guess. I like opera, okay."

Their mother said, "Oh, go get that clipping and show it to Field, will you, honey? You remember the stories in the San Angelo paper last week when Henny Geneson died?"

Field said, "Uh-huh. Aunt Liz's old boyfriend. The famous fighter."

Flannel said, "The New York papers made a big fuss over him—picture on page one of *The Times*. I've got a friend who works for a news magazine, and just for kicks I asked him to check through Geneson's file." Flannel got up. "I brought a couple of the clips home to show Mama." Flannel went off to the back bedroom to get them.

His mother said to Field, "I don't think Flannel ever really believed the stories about poor Liz. But he does now. I told him that the Geneson-Riley fight was all framed right in Liz's New York apartment, and that's why she had to go off to Europe. There were gangsters involved, too. It was just a mess! Did I ever tell you about it?"

"Uh-huh. . . ."

Flannel brought in a couple of photocopies of old newspaper articles and handed them to Field. Henny Geneson had been sued by Elizabeth Lacy, a model, because, she claimed, he failed to marry her as promised. Mrs. Lacy's ex-husband, a Fort Worth, Texas, plumbing contractor, had filed a second action against the fighter, blaming him for the breakup of his marriage.

Field finished a quick reading. "When we were little, you told us that Aunt Liz was married to Geneson."

"Well, honey! She was living with the man! After poor Liz lost her suit he turned right around and married some rich socialite out on Long Island, and that's when Liz went off to Europe. I think he threatened her with gangsters, or they were in on the big gambling that went on and there was supposed to be an investigation of the fight. It was so sordid! Poor Liz. If she hadn't had three husbands in her past, Geneson never could have gotten away with it."

Field stood up. "Aunt Liz is dead, Mama. It's too much ancient history for me. I'm the one who's got to deliver this week's news, remember? You two go right on. I've got to get to the office. What time do you plan to take off?"

Their mother said, "I'm all packed, but I want to take a little bath, and then maybe Flannel and I will stop by the cemetery just to check on Papa's lot. I haven't been by there in a week. We'll still get to Austin in plenty of time for me to get a rest before Banyan plays tonight."

Field nodded to Flannel. "See you there," he said and left.

His mother called after him, "You and Carolyn be careful on the road!" Then Field overheard her say to Flannel, "I think that boy still drives too fast when he's out on the highway."

Every parking place in front of Lady High School had a car in it. He had to park down the street. Every kid has his own car these days, Field thought. It wasn't like that back in the days when he and Keel had gone to school. They had ridden a bus in from the country.

The building had been new then. It was yellow stucco with red tile around the roof line to suggest that the architecture was Spanish in style. The auditorium was in the front and there was a tower that served no function other than decoration. It suggested a bell tower on a Spanish mission, perhaps. Field had been up inside the tower. Keel had told him it was the place to take a girl when you wanted a little action during school hours. You could always hear anyone below on the stairs in plenty of time to pull out and zip up, Keel explained. There had never been a bell. There were no openings at the top at all, just red bricks on the outside where arched openings should have been located.

After the war, two new wings had been added: a science lab and a band practice room. There had been no attempt to match the earlier pseudo-Spanish style. They looked like army barracks. Out in back, the playing field for the Lady High football games had been expanded with rickety scaffolding and board seats.

Field went down the long, central hallway and heard his own footsteps click along the concrete floor. More than forty years ago he had been a student here, and still that old feeling of anxiety returned. Was homework due? The students, restless, looked out of the classrooms to watch him pass.

It had been almost a dozen years now since his own children had gone to school in this building and he and Carolyn had come back for parent conferences. That hadn't cured his distaste for the place.

There were a few black faces in the classrooms now. There had been none when he and Keel were students. It seemed to him that most of the students now were brown. Lady's Latin population was growing. They were the ones who had lots of children, with more and more of them continuing into high school instead of dropping out after the sixth grade to pick cotton or sheer sheep or go to work for the town, digging ditches for the water department or graves in the Lady cemetery.

The secretary in the principal's office was a recent graduate, in a pink sweater that drew Field's eyes to her most prominent features. He smiled. There was a sudden warm feeling inside his thighs. She said, "Hi, Mr. Bonner. How are you today!"

"I'm great—now, Tessie. I can see you're great, too."

She flushed, pinker than the sweater, her eyes bright blue and clear. Her mother was from one of the Swedish families on the ranches out north of Lady. "I'll tell Mr. Webb you're here."

J. J. Webb came out of his office. "Hi, Field. You got your

64

Kodak, I see." Webb was of the generation that called all cameras Kodaks. Field's Nikon was a business expense so he had the best.

"Morning, Mr. Webb."

Tessie said, "I'll go get the girls. Where do you want them?"

Webb looked at Field. "In front of the tower okay? I think we always take them out there, don't we?"

"That's fine," Field said.

Tessie said, "They're already in their uniforms and so excited about having their pictures in the paper. I know they haven't learned a thing all day." She trotted off.

The two men strolled back down the hall, not talking because of the open doors in the classrooms. They passed a room where Field heard a familiar voice saying, "The English language is only a tool, but if you don't treat it with respect and use it properly, it's going to get rusty or, worse still . . ." Miss Dorfoot's voice was a musical chant. Field wondered how after almost fifty years of teaching the same thing year after year she could possibly get any fresh life into her classes.

Outside, Field said, "What was the matter with the Bugs last year, Mr. Webb?"

"Are you asking me that kind of question in your capacity as the newspaperman or do you want a real explanation?"

Field laughed. "Okay. No story yet if you insist. Let's call it an unattributed backgrounder from a highly placed but unidentifiable source."

Behind the uneven hedges surrounding the lower red brick was graffiti: BEAT COLEMAN! JOSE + ANITA, BROWNWOOD SUCKS, EAT THE RICH.

Webb cleared his throat. "I blame Doc right now, if you want to know the truth. He let coach talk him into putting Leroy back into the lineup a week before the boy's knee was okay, and bam, first play against Eden and Leroy was worse off than before. Leroy will be the team this year, pretty much."

"Leroy is all I hear talked about around the square. Some of the guys at the drugstore think he'll go to the university, and there's a bunch that's already got him playing for the Cowboys after that."

65

"It's Doc's responsibility to look out after our boys, and he certainly is well paid for the amount of time he puts in. Doc has gotten so busy with his real-estate deals these days that he hardly seems to have time for the practice of medicine. . . ."

Doc's name keeps coming up, Field thought, as he watched two girls bounce out of the building and come toward them. They were wearing short orange-red skirts, pleated all around. Their satin shirts were orange-red, too, with large black dots, ladybug colors. They carried chromium batons and moved self-consciously, pelvises thrust forward. Webb had been at Lady High, as teacher and then principal, thirty years, and had reached the age when he no longer bothered to remember the students' names. He called all the girls honey. "Honey, this is Mr. Bonner from the newspaper," he said.

Four more girls came out with Tessie, giggling and skipping, happy to be out of classes. There were six cheerleaders in all.

Field asked them to line up, and he handed Tessie his little notebook. "How about writing their names down left to right so I can identify them. There, I'll just grab a couple of quick ones." He shot the lineup and then said, "Okay, everyone stand at attention. Smile. . . ." Click. "Now, everyone jump up in the air when I say jump—keep smiling! On three. One . . . two . . . three . . . jump!" Click. "Let's do it again now." Girl number four had such big breasts that they kept on bouncing after she stopped jumping. It was remarkable. "Let's do it again." The girls had on black underpants and when they came down after a jump there were six pairs of creamy, exposed thighs and satin-covered mounds. Field spotted pubic hairs curling out from under one pair of panties—the girl was the blondest of all. She looked like Tessie, a smaller, younger, plumper Tessie. "Is that your sister?" Field asked.

Tessie smiled. "Of course. We're the famous Olsen girls, and there are lots more where we come from. Our father wanted a boy and he wouldn't give up. Fortunately, he blames Doc and not us."

Field had the girls line up again, three shortest in front of the other three. "Okay, get all your heads in close, and I'm going to

move in close. . . . Let's see your teeth now. Go ahead, laugh."
Click. "That's great. Now, everyone spread out in a big circle and
do your thing with the batons. I'll just shoot up the rest of this
roll. Okay? That's the way. Don't pay any attention to me, but try
not to hit my camera with a baton. Okay?"

They giggled and moved out onto the dry brown lawn and
began to twirl and toss their batons. Field shot a couple of frames
and then knelt down before Tessie's sister. Carolyn had had her
female parts removed at a hospital in San Angelo fifteen years
ago, and she had hinted to him that there would be all the sex he
wanted after that. But right away she began to complain that he
yelled when his legs cramped during the night, and when the last
child left home Field had been moved out of their bedroom.

The next time Tessie's sister jumped up to fling her baton into
the air, he shot her crotch. Suddenly he thought of Keel and all
the girls like this one he had screwed at Lady High and off at the
university and while he was in the navy. Now Keel sent him
photographs of his latest mistress, a girl no older than this one.
Keel had always chased girls and caught them. And Field had
been trapped behind the thick glasses and the thickening midsection and, worst of all, the fear that they would laugh if he made a
pass.

Field turned to see that Tessie was blushing again, bright red,
and he winked at her. He had been caught. Webb apparently
was oblivious to the girls and their love mounds. Field thought,
How does the old man stand it? Surrounded all day by all this
warm, soft, wet, marvelous female sex. Maybe Tessie lets him
have a little. . . . Maybe Webb was an old lady and just didn't
care about such things.

Field finished the roll of film. "Okay, girls, many thanks. That's
it." He suddenly felt keyed up, cheerful.

"When's it going to be in the paper?" one of the girls asked,
thrusting her pelvis up. She was skinny with red kinky hair,
freckles and perfect teeth. Field knew her. He had gone to school
with her mother. "Next Tuesday's edition, unless we get a big rain
over the weekend." In Lady any rain was always the biggest
news possible.

The girls giggled in chorus and were shepherded back into the building by Tessie. "Thanks, Mr. Webb," Field said.

Webb said, "Always glad to cooperate with the press, Field. Can Miss Tompkins get some prints from you for the annual? I know she's going to want some."

"Sure, same as usual. I'll send you a batch."

Webb didn't smile, but he asked, "A complete set?"

The old man wasn't dead after all. "Well, I'll have to edit them a bit. . . ." Field thought, Maybe I'll print up a big one of that blondie's crotch and send it to him. He can hang it in his office. Field said, "I'll be back next month for the basketball team."

"I'll tell the coach you're coming. It won't be as much fun as cheerleaders." He winked.

When Field woke from his nap that afternoon he found his glasses had slipped off his nose, off the couch and onto the floor. The room was a grayed cave. He groped for the glasses, sat up and blinked. What is Doc up to? he thought. He sat, waiting for something to pop into his head, as it sometimes did at moments like this. But nothing came to him at all.

He stopped off in the bathroom at the front of the house and brushed his thinning hair. Carolyn had put a full-length mirror on the inside of his bathroom door so he had to confront daily the paunch that disgusted him. He knew that some men came to love their sagging bellies. He had seen the way they caressed themselves, leaning against the bank building downtown, hugging their guts. They patted themselves in the midsection with obvious fondness.

But Field resented his stomach. It was ugly. That smart ass, skinny Flannel. . . . Keel did sit-ups all the time, the old fool, but Field hated exercise—all exercise. Field pulled in his belt another notch so that it cut into his flesh. There, you fat old fart, he said to the flushed face in the mirror. Suffer.

He got a sudden idea and looked up the telephone number of the hospital.

"Hospital," a woman said.

"Is Doc Allen there this afternoon? This is Field Bonner."

"Oh, Field, this is Mrs. Clardon."

"Yes, ma'am."

"Doc is just down the hall. Do you want to speak to him?"

"Just ask him if he'd like to play nine holes this afternoon. . . ."
Field waited while Mrs. Clardon went to speak to Doc.

"He said I'm not to schedule any patients for whatever time
you say and to tell you to hold up on one until he gets there. Does
all that make sense?"

"Yes, indeed, Mrs. Clardon. I thank you. Tell Doc I'll be there
at four and for him to bring some money."

"I hope you boys don't gamble."

"No, ma'am, Mrs. Clardon. Never."

After he hung up, Field suddenly realized that if he played golf
this afternoon he and Carolyn couldn't possibly drive to Austin in
time to hear Banyan's recital. He shrugged. They would drive to
Austin in the morning. Carolyn could think up some excuse.

Beside the first tee was the pro's hut and three battered aluminum lawn chairs.

Several yards away, down a slope, was a row of rusting, tin-
covered sheds where the regulars kept their golf carts.

By four in the afternoon, the shed was oven hot. Field had
dropped off his film with Mynalou at the office and driven right
out to the golf course. He pulled off his tie and shirt, hung them
on a wire hanger and hooked the hanger over a nail in a rafter.
He pulled on a cotton T-shirt that once had been red but was
now sun-bleached pink, still dark under the arms. He changed
into a pair of old cotton slacks and put on his golf shoes—white
with brown fringe tongues. His spikes pocked the dusty ground.
There were more than two dozen golf caps hanging on the
rafters, most from tourneys he had played in all over Texas, dat-
ing back to his college days when he had worn a green eyeshade
like the ones newspaper copy editors wear in old movies.

In the back of his golf cart was a Styrofoam box. He dumped
in a bag of ice he had brought along. The shed seemed suddenly
hotter.

Field picked up a tall glass of heavy plastic, filled it with ice cubes and poured a generous plop of Wild Turkey into it. There was a holder for the glass on the dashboard of the electric cart. He put his drink there while he backed out and set his cart lurching across the ruts of the trail up to the first tee.

"Hi, ya, Field," Timmy, the pro, said, coming out of his hut to greet him.

Field nodded. He hoped at least three guys from town would show up so the pro wouldn't have to be invited along. Timmy whined when he lost, and he always seemed to lose when Field was in the foursome. Timmy's early promise in Abilene, where he grew up, had not been fulfilled. His game was too erratic. Field heard that the kid smoked a lot of dope, too. It was easy to get Timmy rattled. A kid who was that easy to figure out was no challenge, no fun at all.

Field unwrapped one of his fifty-cent Nicaragua cigars. He remembered the Havanas he used to smoke, cigars he never fully appreciated until they suddenly were gone because of Castro. Keel would bring some cigars. He always did.

Field watched a couple of vehicles, a Cadillac and a pickup, coming out the highway from town. One would be Doc and the other would be Joe Bob. Maybe one of them had brought the judge along.

They wheeled up side by side in clouds of white dust and parked. Joe Bob climbed down out of his pickup and shot a stream of brown slime through his teeth onto the doctor's front tire. "Got to cool 'em down, Doc. You really drive that big fucker, don't you?"

Doc was tall and lean. "He's so clean that he squeaks," was the way Field's mother spoke of him. Doc was married to a formidable woman, a pillar of the Church of Christ, who ran both the music and the preacher there. Doc had a reputation as a ladies' man—like Keel, Field thought.

Joe Bob was short, and his once wiry muscles were thickening into fat. There was more than the beginning of a potbelly. He had taken over his father's business—kitchen appliances, household heaters and liquid gas supply. Joe Bob had a handsome new house, the third one he had built in Lady, and a pretty young wife, also his third. He had a pair of tiny twin daughters by this current wife. He had ex-wives and children in the two other houses he had built in Lady, and he supported all three households. Field's mother thought that Joe Bob and his three wives were one of the more shameful scandals in Lady. "Can you imagine how all those children must feel?" she would ask. "Their daddy has no more morals than a yellow dog. Do you think that he drinks, too?" she would ask Field.

"I imagine he does, Mama," Field would reply easily. Joe Bob's golf cart was red, and his name was painted in script on the side. It had a yellow top with fringe. Today Joe Bob was wearing a bright blue sport shirt and green slacks. He almost always showed up in a new shirt. His wife didn't like to wash his clothes.

Field laughed. His almost silent heh-heh was known to unnerve certain people. "You can't win any other way, so you plan to blind us with those pants of yours, eh, Joe Bob?"

"You are a disgrace, Bonner buddy. A disgrace to the membership of the Lady Golf Club. All the ads that J. C. Penney runs in your miserable newspaper, and you are so cheap you won't even trade with them and buy yourself a respectable golf shirt. You been wearing that sad, faded rag for thirty years that I know of."

Field said, "This is my lucky shirt."

Doc wheeled up silently in his electric cart. A little license plate on the back said M.D. "You got any ice today, Field?"

"Help yourself, Doc."

Joe Bob asked, "Did anybody bring any beer today?"

Timmy said, "I got some Lone Star iced down."

"Goddamnit, don't speak up so fast, Timmy. I got to pay you for your beer. Let me see if I can get a free one off one of these gentlemen first."

Doc said, "I got Scotch, and you know it, Joe Bob. You're welcome to a shot of that."

Joe Bob scowled. "I'm just trying to climb down from a big one. I can't think about hard likker for an hour or so anyway."

Field said, "Go ahead and buy a beer from Timmy. Help the poor kid out. That may be the only money he makes all day, and he'll need it to pay us off if we let him come around with us."

Timmy got Joe Bob a can of Lone Star from the Coke box

71

beside the hut. Doc sat on the back of his cart and changed into his golf shoes. Joe Bob pulled off his boots and instantly was three inches shorter. He had black golf shoes and expensive clubs, custom-made for him because he was so short.

Field poured some more bourbon into his plastic glass and asked, "You line up anybody else, Doc?"

"Smitty said he couldn't make it today. I never saw Leo."

Joe Bob said, "Old pro here is dying to come along. I'd like to see him take some of Field's money, wouldn't you, Doc? God knows I never get to see any of it. I don't know why I keep playing with you boys."

"Nobody else in Lady will put up with your bullshit," Field said softly with a gentle smile. Field had a single fanglike tooth that showed for an instant. Both he and Flannel had the same kind of crooked teeth, inherited from their mother's mother.

Today was so hot that even Doc had beads of sweat on his forehead, and the front of his shirt was dark with dampness.

Timmy was about to tee off. Joe Bob licked the beer off his upper lip. "You giving away any cigars today, Field?"

"Damn moocher," Field said nicely, handing one over.

"O-ooo-e-eee," Joe Bob said as he inspected the band. It was one of the Nicaragua cigars. "I ain't going to set fire to this baby. This one looks good enough to eat. I'm just going to chew her a little bit at a time."

Timmy turned. "Hey, give the kid a break, will you? They don't stand around laughing when Arnie's just getting ready to fire one."

They ignored him. Joe Bob said, "I hear Flannel is home this week."

Field nodded. Word traveled fast in Lady. His mother had already called Aunt Judy who lived just two houses away from Joe Bob's new family. "Keel's coming up. We're meeting in Austin."

Joe Bob said, "Does Flannel really like it up there in New York?"

Field shrugged. "He makes money. Spends it all, of course,

72

trying to stay alive, but a lot of money goes through his hands."

Doc asked, "What's he doing now?"

"Same as always. He works for this big international oil supply outfit. When Shell moved down to Houston he could have moved with them, but he quit because he didn't want to come back and live in Texas. I guess that means he likes it up there, don't you?"

Timmy's drive flew, right down the center of the fairway.

Joe Bob strolled over to push his tee and ball into place. He took a couple of wild swings, uprooted some grass and hunched his shoulders a few times.

Field said evenly, "I bet you two bits you can't get within fifty feet of Timmy's ball."

Joe Bob lowered his club and flushed. "Why, you old fart, if there's one thing I can do it's hit the piss out of a golf ball. Where is his fucking ball? I can't see it."

Timmy said, "I'm about forty yards this side of the green."

Joe Bob's face was red. He said to Field, "You're on. Now, shut the fuck up while I concentrate."

Field turned to Doc. "I got him stirred up now. What can I do that'll get your adrenaline pumping, Doc?"

Doc chuckled just as Joe Bob let loose his mighty swing. The ball flew up and then began to drift over to the left. It dropped rapidly, bouncing crazily on some rocks and skittering off the fairway into the stones that had been placed along the barbed-wire fence.

"Damnit to hell, Doc!" Joe Bob yelled. "You cost me two bits right off the bat. This is going to be an expensive fucking afternoon." His beer can was empty and he flung it away angrily. "Can I have some of your Scotch, Doc?"

Joe Bob and Field had one awful memory in common. In the late twenties a cousin of Thomas Bonner who lived in Brownwood decided to give dancing classes in Lady. She asked Field's mother to enroll him. He learned later that she had wanted Keel, but Keel had turned down the dancing lesson project flat.

Field was nine years old. A whole autumn of Saturday mornings spent tap dancing culminated in a Christmas program. Field,

Joe Bob and three other boys, all dressed as Santas with flopping cotton beards, tapped onto the stage of the high school, went through a noisy routine and then shuffled off to Buffalo. Field could hear his father's laughter even over the piano—even above the rat-ta-ta-tat of the little metal crescents the shoe repairman in the saddle shop had put on the toes of his Sunday shoes.

That was the end of it. Field was mortified and refused to return to the classes after Christmas. None of the other mothers could make their sons go if Field wasn't going, so that spring there were only girls in the dance school. The cousin couldn't afford the expense of driving her car from Brownwood for so few students, and her Lady branch died.

Once many years later at Christmastime, Joe Bob stopped by the newspaper offices to drop off the copy for his holiday ad. No one was in the place but Field. The idea must have just popped into Joe Bob's head, and before he thought it through he began to whistle "Jingle Bells" and broke into the crazy, flopping, arm-swinging tap-dance routine that the little Santas had done thirty years earlier.

Field grinned, but his feeling of terrible embarrassment burned again. When Joe Bob saw Field's reaction, he, too, turned red and his eyes flashed in anger. He dropped his papers on the counter and muttered, "Goddamn little faggots!" and fled. Joe Bob, skinny and twitching with nervousness, had been the best dancer of them all. And he had loved it.

This afternoon it may have been the bouncing way Joe Bob moved toward the green on the fourth hole that made Field remember the Christmas program. As Joe Bob passed him, Field softly whistled "Jingle Bells" through his teeth so that only Joe Bob could hear it.

Then Field smiled and sipped his bourbon, leaning against his golf cart. Just as Joe Bob got ready to hit the ball he looked back at Field. Joe Bob's face was red, and he swung at the ball with such fury that it sliced up crazily to the right and, although he was only twenty-five feet away, missed the green entirely.

Doc was puzzled by the sudden display of anger and rage that followed. Doc said, "You better stop by my office and let me check you out one of these days, Joe Bob. Your motor's running awfully fast."

Doc's game was going well. It was the best that Field had ever seen him play. By the sixth hole, Doc was out in front by four strokes. The pro and Field were even and Joe Bob trailed, cursing, in an increasingly bad mood as his number of strokes climbed. He was bumming bourbon from Field now.

They were waiting for Joe Bob to get himself out of a sand trap. He was yelling at an innocent horned toad that had scurried across the sand just as he was getting ready to hit the ball. "They got horns like the devil himself!" Joe Bob said.

Field poured himself a fresh bourbon, added some ice and went over to lean against Doc's cart.

Joe Bob screamed, "Cut out rattling that ice, Field, you fucker!"

Field said, "You ever see anybody die of high blood pressure out on the golf course, Doc?"

"Not this week."

Field said, "Hey, I saw old Webb at the high school this afternoon, and you'll be glad to know he places all the blame for the Bugs' poor showing last fall squarely on your shoulders."

Doc looked up quickly and Field knew that he had hit on a sensitive subject. "The poor old man's got to pass around the blame or it's his ass. Coach is in too solid with the Bug boosters after year before last. He's got a year or two of grace."

Doc said evenly, "Well, just how in the hell did Webb link me to the boys' miserable showing against Calf Creek?"

"Oh, it's that big black boy. Webb says you let him play again before his injury was healed, and now he may be out again for another season."

Doc closed his eyes as if in pain. He dug his club into the ground at his feet. "Let him play! Those stupid assholes!"

Field pretended slight shock. "Hey, Doc, I didn't know you even knew words like that."

Timmy said, "Joe Bob took at least eight strokes for that hole, but he gave himself a six. Are we going to let him get away with it?"

Joe Bob yelled, "You don't count it when I was just pushing

75

rocks away from in front of the ball with my club! That's legal!"

They rode their carts over to tee off on the seventh.

Field sidled up to Doc and said quietly, "I feel lucky on this hole. I know it's got your name on it, but five says you don't make par."

Doc always shot three on this hole. It was a snap for him. He sometimes did it in two. "You're on," he said.

Joe Bob had overheard. "Can I get in on this one, Field? This is Doc's hole. He never misses. I can't make any money on myself this afternoon, that's for fucking sure."

Field nodded. "All right. How much you want?"

"Hell, I'll go for five, too. Doc and I will wipe that goddamn grin off your face."

Just as Doc moved up to fire off the ball from the tee, Field said to Timmy, "Have you noticed how this town has got the most rabid bunch of football fans in Texas?"

Doc's drive hooked and fell well short of the green.

Joe Bob let out a string of curses. "Jesus, Doc! I was counting on you! You owe me some Scotch on that one."

Doc not only didn't make par on the hole, Field did it in two and cut Doc's lead to two.

Field was calm on the surface, but inside he felt his excitement rising. He had rarely bothered with Doc in the past. Doc's game usually was so mediocre that Field could beat him handily. And Doc always took his golf casually, or seemed to.

They were walking side by side, back to their golf carts. "You a bit edgy today, Doc?" Field asked cheerfully. There was no answer. "Here, you still got the best score going. You don't want to mess it up now. . . ."

Doc climbed into his cart and turned it sharply away as he started off. "I know what you're doing, Field. You shit—"

Ah, Doc was getting mad. Still, the name-calling made Field feel a flash of anger. The arrogant bastard. Keel acted like that sometimes.

The eighth hole, except for a small clump of live oak trees in the middle of the fairway, was perfectly straightforward. It had a par three. If the ball went over the trees, the hole held no real problems at all. The green was banked so that it faced the golfer as he approached. The traps were all behind the green, a penalty for overshooting. Because of some scraggly trees that had grown too tall, eight had become a blind tee hole, and there was a certain suspense in finding out where the ball had landed after the first shot.

Joe Bob led off, blasting up a cloud of dust and dead grass. His ball sailed almost straight up and then sank out of sight. But it had cleared the trees.

Timmy's ball sailed just over the trees in a clean, smooth arc. Joe Bob said, "That's cutting it a bit close, don't you think?"

Timmy said, "I got this one figured out exactly. Numero ocho is my lucky number. I usually birdie here."

Field heh-heh-hehed. Timmy looked sheepish.

Doc was trying to jam his sharp aluminum tee into the rough clods of clay and dead weeds.

Field said, "Hey, Doc, I was in your drugstore having coffee with old Milt this morning, and we were talking about how nice it was of old lady Codder to leave you her place when she died last summer. . . ."

Doc straightened up slowly. His tee was crooked, but it held the ball. He took his stance. Were his hands shaking?

Field watched closely. Doc's face seemed a bit pale, didn't it? Field sipped his bourbon and smiled to himself.

Doc jerked his arms back and up and then slashed at the ball with a furious stroke. The ball fell off the tee and rolled a few inches. Joe Bob burst out laughing. "Jesus H. Christ! You trying to kill that poor little thing, Doc?"

"Shut your fucking face," Doc said to Joe Bob, picking up the ball, straightening the tee and getting ready to try again. This time he made solid contact, but the ball failed to climb. Instead, it hit a big rock about twenty yards out, shot up into the air and then dropped into the trees beyond.

Field didn't smile, but suddenly he felt a nice calmness in his chest. He pressed in his tee and ball, polished his driver absently on his pants leg while he looked at the fairway. He thought of

Keel at that moment. Keel had never learned to play golf. He was chasing pussy. When Field hit the ball he didn't even have to watch it to know that it flew flawlessly above the trees. It might even be on the green. Joe Bob whistled in admiration.

Field followed Doc again. They got off their carts and walked together to the trees. Field said, "I'll help you find your ball, Doc."

Doc made a grunting sound. There was brush as well as tree trunks, and Doc's ball finally was found under a small thorny shrub. Field said, "Damn, Doc, that's too bad. Just when you had a real score going for you, too. Why don't you just pick it up and throw it out of here? The other guys are way up there. They won't know."

Doc said, "You think I'm a cheater?" His eyes were hot with fury.

Field smiled slowly, easily. "Shit, Doc, nobody who is as nice to old ladies as you are is going to try to trim off a few strokes. You and I know that."

Doc hit at the ball. It went into the slender trunk of a live oak and bounced crazily into some cactus. He had to kick aside one of the plants to get at his ball, and it took two more strokes just to get out of the trees. Field chuckled sympathetically. "If you can just get the town to go along with putting up a new hospital out there on that land you got now, you're going to make a piss pot full of money, aren't you, Doc?"

Field was watching him closely. Doc turned white around the mouth. He was grinding his teeth. "You shit," he said in a hoarse voice, "I'll ruin you. I'll take over that goddamn pile of puerile crap you call a newspaper, and I'll run you out of town!"

Field had pushed too hard. He had overplayed it a bit. Shot three bullets when a single would have done the job. But he knew that he had won, and Doc knew that Field was onto his game. Field held up a placating hand. "Now, Doc, don't—" He wasn't really worried about Doc hitting him. Field was big and he knew he looked solid. He hadn't had a fight since he was a teenager, and that had been with Keel, of course.

Joe Bob, up ahead on the eighth green, yelled, waving his arms

78

wildly, pointing and holding up a single finger. They had found Field's ball. His drive had gone into the cup. It was a hole in one.

It took a few seconds before Doc in his fury realized what had happened to the game. Then he flung his club off in the direction of the trees, turned and stalked across the ditch and the cart trail, leaving the game, leaving his cart and the other golfers standing there watching him march away. Doc climbed into his Cadillac and sent up a cloud of dust as he wheeled it back to the highway and into town.

Joe Bob began laughing, a crazy, drunken hooting so loud that Field heard it following him as he walked back to his cart.

Field drove up to the green and walked over to see his ball in the cup. Field had made a hole in one on eight once before, back in 1946. How many rounds had he played between that time and this? Say, three hundred rounds a year maybe since then . . . must be thousands. Field smiled to himself, retrieved his ball and drove his cart bumpily along, sipping his bourbon. Maybe he'd let himself smoke an extra cigar as a reward. Doc was in his pocket now. There might be a new hospital or not. Now Field could decide. He had the man.

Timmy put Doc's clubs back into their bag. He would return them and Doc's abandoned cart to the shed.

Back at the cart garage, Joe Bob started in laughing again. The sun was burning out in the west. The moon was a big white golf ball up in the eastern sky. They changed their clothes and walked together up the rutted hill to the parking place.

"That Doc," Field said, "he sure is a pisspoor sportsman. He doesn't know how to play the game at all, does he, Joe Bob?"

THREE

Horner Bonner

HORNER and his wife walked along the flagstone path under the huge, moss-hung oaks. The night was warm and sticky, and Ellie's silver hair had just undergone fifty dollars worth of teasing and lacquer. She wanted to get it into air conditioning quickly.

By this time on a Friday evening Horner was tired. Ellie, on the other hand, was twitching with energy. She had played tennis at the club all morning and then slept after lunch. As she got to the door, she asked, "Are you all right, baby?"

"Maybe a drink will get me going."

"Eat some of the crackers when they come around, will you remember? Did you eat lunch today?"

"I had diet biscuits. You told me not to eat lunch, remember?"

She patted him on the arm as they stepped into the pool of light at the front door. "Easy, baby. I'll watch out for you, and everything will be okay. Take it easy on the salt now."

Horner pressed the button and heard the chimes inside. A dog began to bark. Then a second dog joined in. Horner said, "Why don't they send those beasts away when they entertain?"

Teelee opened the door. Her cries of greeting were piercing. The women hugged each other. They had been students at Stephens twenty-five years before and friends ever since. Teelee was married to the publisher of *The Houston News*.

Countess, an old Great Dane with a rotting tail, jumped up on

Horner, slobbering on his navy blue suit. Teelee was horrified. "Oh, you bad dog! Gordon! Come get Countess, will you?"

Gordon Jordan came through the arched opening into the entrance hall. A fat bulldog waddled after him. Gordon was several inches taller than six feet and so thin that Horner always thought of his brother Flannel. Gordon grinned and kicked at Countess, kissed Ellie on the cheek and patted her on the behind with one hand while he shook Horner's hand with the other. "My God, you look ravishing, Ellie," he said. "Evening, Horner. Get out, Countess!" Gordon was already well along with the evening's drinking—relaxed, shuffling, happy. He had on a pair of gray snakeskin boots. They added at least three more inches to his already remarkable height.

The living room was a huge cavern. Teelee had made the curtains and slipcovers herself from printed bed sheets that were a blaze of gigantic green and purple flowers. There were three sofas, six odd chairs, three footstools of various styles and shapes and a dozen tables, none matching. Teelee was very snobbish about the fact that she wouldn't let a decorator inside her house. Horner had noted that when she entertained, she often spent most of the evening pushing footstools around, insisting that everyone be comfortable on furniture that made comfort impossible.

She introduced Horner and Ellie to an ancient couple with matching drinks who were sitting side by side on one of the sofas. The man was B. Hank Bodie, a Texas literary celebrity.

The sight of the impressive, hawk-nosed profile gave Horner a moment of panic. Horner once had signed up for Bodie's famous course at the university and had dropped out from utter boredom. Early in his career Bodie had published a book about women in Texas and their role in its settlement. The book eventually had made Bodie something of a darling of the local women's movement. It was ironic, since he treated his wife abominably, humiliating her at every opportunity. Horner had heard a long time ago that in fact it had been Bodie's wife who had done all the research and most of the writing on *Women of Our West*. Teelee once said that if Bodie had ever read his own book and found out how sympathetic it was to women he would have been furious.

Horner said, "Of course, we know Dr. Bodie, Teelee. I took his course at the university years ago, and I think we probably have met since then, too."

Ellie said, "I read your piece in the *News* every Sunday, Dr. Bodie. Everything I know about Texas I've learned from you. I just don't know where on earth you pick up all your fascinating information."

The old man tried to smile.

Horner hoped he wouldn't get stuck at the dinner table beside Mrs. Bodie. She looked mean, too.

Gordon brought Ellie a glass of wine and handed Horner a bourbon and water. Horner wrapped his hand around the icy glass and felt better instantly. It made him wonder for a moment if he were an alcoholic. He would have to try doing without a drink for a day or two and see if abstinence made him jittery. Maybe he would cut back tonight. Just this one before dinner. The Jordans always served wine with dinner, and that was where he got into trouble. He sipped his bourbon. It was strong. Gordon had skipped the water, the bastard. Horner decided he would just hold the drink for a while and let some of the ice melt. Ellie was chattering away.

When a pause occurred, Horner smiled and said to Dr. Bodie, "I have a mental image of this drink going down and turning my stomach into stone. Do you remember the old demonstrations against alcohol, Dr. Bodie?" The old man looked confused, but Mrs. Bodie nodded encouragingly. Horner said, "When I was a kid, one of those traveling preachers came through my hometown and stopped off at our church—to give a demonstration about the evils of drink. All the Sunday-school classes were sent into the auditorium. He had three jars and three pieces of raw beef. First he gave a spiel about how when we drink water everything is just fine, and he dropped one piece of the meat into the water. It sank slowly. He poured a Coke into the second jar, and when he dropped in the meat, the Coke boiled up around it, and he said that the Coke was cooking the meat and that Coke cooks our insides the same way. Next, he said there was alcohol in the third jar, and he passed around a dark rock that he said was meat that had been dropped into alcohol—he never said how long it had been in—"

Ellie interrupted. "Sometimes I think you tell that story every time you take a drink, Horner."

Dr. Bodie looked blank, but Mrs. Bodie was delighted. She said, "I hope you won't mind if Dr. Bodie uses your little story in his Sunday column one of these days?"

Horner laughed. "I don't think Gordon would be too happy if you tried. I'm sure that Coke is an advertiser, and Gordon's newspaper is full of ads for booze. He wouldn't print that story at all."

Mrs. Bodie seemed puzzled. "But it's a charming story—old folklore and all that. We could interview a chemist. . . . I'll go ask Gordon right now. . . ." She hopped up and went off to find him, but Gordon was busy in the front entranceway, greeting more guests and bringing them in for Teelee to introduce around. At least six couples, twelve strangers, Horner thought with some dismay. I'll never keep them straight.

He finished his drink and rattled the ice. The host heard it.

The bourbon was working nicely. Gordon took Horner's glass right out of his hand and filled it again. Horner drank that, too. By the time Teelee announced dinner, he was fairly numb.

Mrs. Bodie turned up on one side of him at the table and the young wife of an architect was on the other. Mrs. Bodie talked happily to herself. The young woman was named Ann. Ellie had whispered earlier that she was rumored to be Gordon's current girlfriend. Horner wondered aloud: "Why aren't there ever any rumors about my girlfriends?" Ellie, horrified, scurried away.

Horner had to concentrate on the table in front of him. The silverware was the real thing, heavy and ornate. There were tiny flowers all over Teelee's china, and real flowers, tiny, too, in vases down the center of the table. The pale green soup was salty. Teelee jumped up to help the black woman remove the bowls.

Horner thought solemnly, This is so awful, and I am so tired that I wish I were home in bed asleep.

The girl next to him was saying, "Oh, it's such a good movie! You know, they just don't make movies like that anymore, and Olivier, well, he is just the most beautiful hunk . . ."

Gordon leaned over his plate at the head of the table and said to her, "Are you talking about me, Ann?" Then he added a sort of booming crash of a laugh that stopped all other talk at the table.

Teelee jumped right in. "Oh, my, but we are jolly tonight, aren't we?" Everyone laughed and conversations picked up again.

Horner tried to explain who he was in answer to a question from Ann. He insisted that he was Mr. Dull himself. "I work for a big law firm. No, it isn't the least bit exciting. We do handle some of the big real-estate transactions around Houston. . . . Why shouldn't Arabs buy buildings in Houston if they can afford them? The Germans, too. We have to get some of that oil money coming back this way, don't we?"

The dining room took on a golden tint. Horner began to notice how beautiful the women were. Across from him old man Bodie's white hair caught Horner's attention for a minute, and Horner thought of his own father. Then in the nice alcohol haze, he recalled sadly that his father was dead. His mother had said, "I'm not sure that you and Flannel really knew your father the way the older boys did—when he was younger and more fun. He was such a cutup."

Horner thought she must be crazy to have forgotten. After Flannel had gone off to college and then to the Navy, Horner had had their father all to himself for five years. And they had played jokes on each other during that whole time. During those years Horner would get into a hot shower and stand for hours. His father once sneaked in with a big pan full of cold water and threw it over the top of the shower curtain. Horner screamed with surprise and shock, and his father laughed until he had to lie down.

Two mornings later, Horner did the same thing to his father. His mother had said, "Now, what if your poor father had a heart attack, Horner!" but she was giggling.

The talk across the table from Horner was about some performance of the Houston opera. No one seemed to expect Horner to comment on musical events. Then the conversation turned to politics—as it always did at the Jordans' house. But Horner had picked up something from the earlier conversation that intrigued him. He asked, "You mean she was singing up there on the stage with no clothes on at all?"

Teelee said instantly, "Don't you sing in the shower, Horner?" and got a big laugh.

The dinner plates were large with gold rims. There were candles in silver holders on the table with the bouquets. . . . The flowers were in cut-glass bowls. Horner's mother had some cut glass displayed in a bookcase in the living room. There was one glass that was partly red. It had been Horner's father's drinking glass when his father was a child, a gift from his Aunt Ida Lou. Horner had a photograph of his father at the age of nine, a tiny, skinny boy with big ears, dressed in a suit, but barefoot, in a photographer's studio in front of a painted backdrop of palm fronds, standing next to a piano stool. Horner's mother said, "The man next door to your grandfather's home was a photographer. He felt sorry for your father when his mother died, so he took dozens of wonderful pictures of him. I thought you might like to have this one."

Once when Horner was a teenager he had worked for a summer on a road construction crew. They built a concrete bridge across Lost Creek on the highway to Voca. The work gang called Horner "Angel Ears." After long hair became stylish, Horner always had the barber leave his hair heavy over the ears to help disguise their astonishing size.

The girl named . . . What was her name? . . . Ann. Ann interrupted his thoughts by asking, "What on earth are you thinking about, with that sad look on your face?"

"Ears," explained Horner.

"Oh!" she shrilled, laughing wildly, as if he had said something remarkably funny. "That's wonderful! I mean, here we are drinking some twenty-dollar-a-bottle wine, and you're wishing you had beer. That kind of honesty is so refreshing."

"No," Horner said, "I said ear."

She pulled back. "Ear? But that's not funny. That doesn't even make any sense. Everyone told me you were supposed to be so funny, Clayton."

"My name is Horner. I'm Horner Bonner."

"Bonner! You don't by any chance have a brother in New York?"

Horner nodded. "That's Flannel."

"Flannel! Tall and thin with lots of black hair?"

"It's getting gray now."

"My mother used to know him. She used to talk about him all the time. He's some kind of worried genius, she would say. You know, your family has a reputation for being the most terrible snobs. And honestly, growing up in a town like Lady! Don't you come from Lady? I've never understood what on earth you have to be snobbish about."

"I don't think we're snobs. We're just small-town boys. I got the hell out of Lady as soon as I could."

"What's Flannel doing now? I'll have to tell Mother."

"He works for an oil supply outfit, some kind of engineering firm in New York."

"I thought he had something to do with show business?"

"He's helped produce a couple of shows off Broadway. He gets his name in the paper sometimes."

"Oh, but that's so exciting! The theater! Famous actors. The Great White Way! I think I ought to give New York a chance, don't you?"

Horner realized suddenly that she was even drunker than he— a disgusting condition for a woman, especially one so young and pretty. She talked on, a blur of face and voice.

A new plate was put before him. Eat, he thought. That's the only way you'll get through this evening alive. "Excuse me," he said politely to Ann and turned his attention to his plate. He ate seriously for a few minutes. It was some kind of meat in gray sauce over noodles. Not bad. Maybe he was just hungry. He hadn't had any lunch, after all. All that drinking on a practically empty stomach . . . No wonder he had come close to disgracing himself.

Now, if he could just make it to coffee. . . . Setting goals like that in life helped, he thought. Even little goals.

Later in the living room, he explained to Gordon, as he had for years, that brandy gave him a most piercing headache. Teelee brought him a tall glass of orange juice. "Teelee, you are one of the world's most magnificent women," he told her, and he meant it. She patted his cheek. Usually, he was afraid of Teelee.

He talked to some of the other guests, although he was uncertain who they were. One vague woman had a thick French accent that seemed to captivate Ellie. Everything that he could think of to say seemed disjointed, out of sync.

A fat man in an expensive, pinstriped suit asked, "Why does a woman have two holes close together?"

Teelee said, "I don't think I ought to hear this."

The fat man yelled, "So you can pick 'em up and carry 'em like a six-pack of beer!"

The women who heard him cried out in protest. "Gross! Gross!" But there was drunken laughter, too.

Someone else asked why it took two Aggies to eat an armadillo. "One eats it while the other watches out for cars."

"Ugh! Awful!" the women cried. But there was laughing, too, and more Aggie jokes. Gordon came over and repeated some terrible puns he had heard. He seemed to have an unlimited supply.

Keep your eyes open, Horner kept telling himself. But he felt his torso slump in Teelee's antique Windsor rocker that belonged in a museum. It had been Teelee's great-grandmother's chair, and the legs were very short. A piece of wood that held the spokes together pressed painfully into his back.

Horner was completely out of things when Ellie finally told him it was time for them to go. He managed to mumble something to Teelee, and, because two or three other couples were at the front door leaving at the same time, Horner got out the door with just a wink at Gordon.

When he was drunk, Gordon tended to hug everyone in a lingering farewell, regardless of sex.

Horner woke at five thirty the next morning even though it had been after one when they got home from the Jordans'. He always woke early. He slipped out of his side of the big bed, pulled on a pair of old shorts and padded down the hall to the kitchen. He put on water for coffee and then went to the front of the house to see if the paper was on the lawn. Not yet. On Saturdays it often was late.

Horner wandered back to the kitchen. He leaned over the sink, drank from his palm and then spit the water out. The taste in his mouth was awful. He decided that he felt terrible. How much had he drunk last night? He didn't want to think about last night. He couldn't remember driving home at all.

He took his coffee out onto the deck in the rear of their house where the property overlooked a deep bayou. They had landscaped a trail down to the dull brown water. Their neighbors on each side had added swimming pools, half hanging out in space over the sharp slope down to the bayou. Ellie had put in oleanders, castor beans and elephant ears, a jungle of plants, to screen off the construction forms that supported the neighbors' pools. The children had begged for a pool, too, but with all the expenses of sending them to college, there never seemed to be enough money. Now that they were gone, off on their own, Ellie thought she'd rather have the little bit of backyard for a garden. There was always the club if they wanted to go swimming.

Horner was startled by her voice behind him. "Are you crazy, just sitting here like that? We have to be out at the airport in less than an hour!"

"We what!"

"We accepted an invitation to go to an art opening in Little Rock this afternoon, and the deRian plane leaves this morning at seven thirty."

"Little Rock? Little Rock, Arkansas? When did you accept? I can't even stand up this morning, Ellie. I think I'm sick."

"Last night at Teelee's. Mme. deRian asked us, and you said you thought it sounded interesting."

"I did?"

"You mean to sit there and tell me you don't remember the conversation?"

"Why on earth should we fly all the way to Little Rock?"

"That's where the exhibit is. Dubuffets—you know, the man with eyes in the sky and bowler hats. Or is that Magritte? Anyway, you told Mme. deRian that you thought Magritte was funny, and she decided on the spot that you are some kind of art expert and that you must go see this exhibit she has arranged in Little Rock."

Horner struggled up from the aluminum and plastic lounge chair. The plastic stuck to his bare back, a sensation he detested. "Jesus, Ellie. I've got to quit drinking! I don't remember any of it. Which one was Mrs. deRian? Can't you call it off? Phone her and say that I'm sick."

"At six in the morning? Never. Besides, I want to go. I think we ought to do it. Let's get a move on."

Horner followed her through the house and into their bedroom. He threw his shorts at the bed and headed for the shower. "Did you pick up my brown suit at the cleaners?"

"It's not supposed to be ready until today." She sat at her dressing table, absorbed by the business of painting her mouth.

"Will a blazer be okay for an art exhibit?" he shouted.

"We're having lunch at Winrock, too."

"What? I can't hear you."

"Get out of there, and let's go!" she yelled.

Through the noise of the water, Horner caught only the hysteria in her voice, not her words. This was going to be one of Ellie's nervous days.

The deRian planes flew out of the old Houston airport where their international construction company had its own hangar, with a parking lot reserved for its executives and their guests.

A young woman in a pinafore greeted them inside the hangar where there was a windowed waiting area. "Oh, you must be the Bonners. I'm so glad that you could join us at the last moment. Our other passengers will be along in just a moment, I'm sure."

Ellie asked, "Is Mme. deRian here yet?"

"Oh, she's not going with us this morning. She spent most of the week in Little Rock putting the exhibit together, and now she's on her way to New York for a party they are giving at their apartment there this evening."

Horner asked, "There's more than one company plane?"

"There are three at the moment. We're going to Little Rock in the old one, I'm afraid. Let's see, we're going to be eighteen in all in our party. Here come the others now."

An orange school bus stopped outside. The rest of the party came filing into the waiting room. They were all men, and all of them were dressed in black suits. They were priests, sixteen of them, Catholic priests in all shapes and sizes and ages, joking and laughing together like children off on a holiday trip. Horner looked sideways at Ellie and saw her trying to cover up her astonishment with a smile of greeting.

"Fathers," the young woman announced cheerfully, "this is Mr. and Mrs. Bonner. You must introduce yourselves, but we need to get right on board because it's almost time for us to be in the air, and the pilot's ready to take off."

Ellie said under her breath, "Jesus, what will they do to this poor little old Baptist girl when they get her up in the air?"

Horner said, "Wash her mouth out with soap."

They filed up the steps into the belly of the plane. The priests were shaking hands with the Bonners and explaining that they were faculty members at the University of St. James. The deRians often included them on such outings. Madame was devoted to St. James and occasionally put together art exhibits especially for the university. There was one priest along, however, from St. B's Church, as he called it. He had a reputation for being interested in art, he explained, so Madame had included him on this trip.

Ellie whispered to Horner, "Hasn't he the most beautiful eyelashes you've ever seen?"

He said his name was Father Cranshaw, and when he saw the effect he was having on Ellie he said, "Why not come sit by me, Mrs. Bonner? I like to sit right up front where we can see what the pilots are up to. They'll open the door as soon as we're in the air, and we can watch everything."

Horner nodded them on and moved into a seat next to a window over the wing.

An enormously fat priest came in after him, his huge red ham of a hand outstretched, his jowls quivering. "I'm Father O'Neal, and I'm hot. Okay if I sit next to you, Mr. Bonner?"

93

"Certainly," Horner said. "And please call me Horner."

"Horner? As in the nursery rhyme? What kind of a Christian name is that?" He laughed to show he was just kidding.

Horner watched out of the corner of his eye as the priest took off his jacket. The man was sweating profusely, and he smelled rancid. Under the jacket was a black dickey with a tight white collar. O'Neal loosened it so that it flopped down halfway onto his massive pink chest. His nipples sagged on breasts like those of an old woman, but there was a heavy mat of damp gray hair. Horner turned away to hide his disgust.

The woman in the pinafore was a kind of stewardess. She came and took Father O'Neal's black jacket from him. She said, "Let's all fasten our seat belts so we can get right into the air. You're expected for lunch at Winrock, and we don't want to make you late."

O'Neal was having difficulty getting the seat belt expanded enough to fasten around his enormous belly. Horner watched him, determined not to laugh or show his dismay. The priest got redder. The sweat ran down from his forehead. He began to laugh, a huge, happy laugh that came up from his belly. "I guess it's about time I began to practice a little girth control," he said.

The plane landed on Winrock's private airstrip. Horner recalled that Winthrop Rockefeller, the former Arkansas governor, had died a few years ago. It turned out that no Rockefellers were in residence at the moment. It was all vague. They were greeted at the house by a handsome woman who said she was the house-keeper. She had servants bring drinks into the living room with its glass-walled view of splendid, rough mountains all around.

Ellie's priest went immediately to the grand piano, sat down and began playing "Love for Sale" in a smooth, improvised style that would have set the perfect mood in a posh cocktail lounge. Ellie, who had been annoyed first that Mrs. deRian wasn't on the plane and now because there were no Rockefellers to greet her, brightened. She whispered to Horner, "He really is the most charming man, and listen to that! He plays the piano like a dream! I may convert."

94

Horner nodded. "Feel free."

The hostess came over to him. "Since you're the only man with his collar on the right way you must be Mr. Bonner."

"Yes . . . I am—" He paused, but she remained silent, smiling expectantly. He said, "I've been admiring your view. This is my first time in Arkansas, and it has a unique look I hadn't expected. The mountains aren't at all like ours out in West Texas."

"There is a poetic roughness, I like to think, a little more vegetation probably than you have in Texas. . . ."

A man in a white jacket came with a drink. Horner realized he wanted it, needed it. That was a bad sign, wasn't it? But just having a cold glass in his hand made him relax a bit, even before he took a sip.

"You're a lawyer in Houston?"

He sipped. "Yes, I handle real estate mostly. It's just paperwork. I never get to see the buildings, and they all belong to other people—not me." He smiled.

"But Houston is such a boomtown. You have the right kind of practice, I should think." She was bored. Her eyes were wandering. "If you'll excuse me, I'll go see if our lunch is ready."

Ellie's priest had slipped smoothly into "Tea for Two." She was leaning over the enormous grand, humming along. He was encouraging her.

By drinking very quickly and moving adroitly in a direction ahead of the waiter, Horner managed to get a second drink.

They were called into the dining room. The housekeeper sat at the head of the table; a large formal luncheon was served in several courses. The priests were all jolly. The housekeeper and Ellie had plenty of attention.

As the sherbet was being served, the housekeeper cleared her throat. The table fell silent. A peacock screamed crazily somewhere outside. The housekeeper said, "Mrs. Rockefeller wanted me to tell you how sorry she is that she couldn't be with you for lunch today. Since Mme. deRian called just a couple of days ago, Mrs. Rockefeller found she was unable to cancel her plans for a board meeting in Hot Springs this afternoon. But she asked me to extend to you the hospitality of Winrock. This is a working ranch,

I'm sure you know. And, since we've found that most visitors have a genuine curiosity about our beef-breeding program, I've asked the Winrock veterinarian to stand by out in the barns. You have a little time before you have to fly on to Little Rock, so if you've finished your coffee, Estelle will show you out to the barns. . . ."

Estelle was a sober young woman in a long white medical jacket, standing in the doorway.

The priests crowded around the housekeeper, delivering effusive thanks. They were pros at that sort of thing. Ellie disappeared down the hall to repair her makeup. Horner desperately wanted a nap. His father had slept for fifteen minutes after lunch every day of his life, then bounced up and gone cheerily back to work. Horner moved around the table to Ellie's place and drank her coffee. She never finished any drink. She never cleaned a plate of food. Once when he had pointed this out to her, she said, "People will think you grew up poor if you don't leave a little something. Didn't you know that?"

The barns were white and looked as if they had just been freshly painted. The party was ushered into an amphitheater. It was sometimes an operating room. Horner thought he had never seen facilities quite so splendid, and yet behind him he heard Ellie saying to her priest, "My husband grew up on a ranch. This sort of thing is just his cup of tea."

Everyone stood around. The vet, a young man with a big black mustache and wearing a long white smock, pointed up to a large, framed photograph of a stupendous bull hung on the wall. The bull's most prominent features, after the mass of poundage that made up his chest, were his enormous balls, hanging down in their bright pink sack. Horner felt a sudden embarrassment, with all the priests standing around, seeing the bull's vivid equipment. Balls meant sex, and priests didn't have anything to do with that, did they?

The vet was delivering what sounded very much like a memorized speech. Horner tuned in and caught on that this bull the vet was talking about was dead—had been dead for five years.

". . . and in our special freezing units here at Winrock we have enough of his sperm to last several more years."

Since old Prince Hal's death—with the help of the Winrock staff—he had continued to sire hundreds of calves, far more per season than when he was alive and in his prime. "The controls that we have established in this lab," the vet continued, "have made it possible to keep a close check on all Prince Hal's off-spring, both those that are sired here at Winrock and those on other ranches where Hal's sperm is purchased for the herds. . . ."

But had Prince Hal enjoyed servicing cows when he was alive? Or was it just a chore for animals? Horner looked around and saw that all the jolly priests had solemn faces now, and Horner wondered if they were searching around in their theological educations for precedents that would put this information into some kind of perspective. Imagine, a hundred immaculate conceptions a year. Prince Hal, the father, long gone from this world, but still a kind of immortal sire, reproducing as long as the icebox kept his sperm fertile. A hundred virgin heifers, attended by angels in white medical robes with syringes and the holy sperm . . .

Horner noticed that Ellie was frowning at him. He must have been smiling to himself. She apparently thought that this was serious business, that he mustn't turn it into some kind of dirty joke by laughing.

Winrock's style was completely foreign to the breeding that had gone on when Horner was growing up. He was fourteen when Flannel was drafted. Keel was a lieutenant in the navy. Field was in the army in North Africa or maybe on the way to the landing in Sicily. Banyan was stationed out in California. There was no one available for hire to do work on a ranch, no one at all.

And Horner, left at home, had five years of listening to his mother worry aloud about not getting letters, about putting to-gether packages to mail overseas, of trying to get enough sugar so she could can her peaches. War news with any mention of casual-ties triggered her hot flashes. His mother, wild-eyed in her meno-pausal frenzy, would whisk up her skirt and begin fanning her face.

They had one Jersey milk cow for the family, and Horner looked after her. Once a year he and his father led her next door to be impregnated by a neighbor's Hereford bull. Horner's father paid twenty-five dollars for the service with the understanding that if no calf resulted, he would get his money back.

But the big Hereford never failed. Horner liked to watch these matings. The bull never wasted any time. But there was none of the wild abandon that frightened Horner when horses coupled. In spite of his weight, the bull was surprisingly agile in the way he threw himself up onto Aida's back.

Horner's mother named cows after her favorite operas. Tosca had died when a rattlesnake bit her in the lip as she was grazing. Horner named the calves. And the spring he was fifteen, he named his most memorable calf after a U.S. fighter plane that was supposed to end the war all by itself. The newly born calf, stumbling around the cow lot, began to run. Suddenly all four feet left the ground at once. "Look, Papa," Horner yelled, "he can fly! This one can fly like a P-40."

The name stuck, and P-40 became a legend.

Horner, who did the milking before and after school, had to compete from the first with the growing young bull for Aida's milk. By April, P-40 had a couple of hard buttons where his horns were beginning to sprout. He and Horner would play together, butting each other and then scampering away. One day Horner's mother complained that Aida's milk production seemed to be falling off drastically.

"Well, P-40 needs a little milk to wash down that awful dry feed."

"You come back to the house with at least three gallons in the bucket tonight before you let that P-40 into the lot. You hear me, Horner?"

"He stands outside the fence and cries if he hears his milk hit the side of the can."

"It isn't his milk! Remember, Horner—three gallons tonight, and more every night until P-40 is weaned."

"He'll hurt Aida."

"You get a stick and hit him if he does."

The next day, P-40 broke down the fence before Horner got home from school. Horner's mother, when she heard the boards to the cow-lot fence breaking, rushed out, but she couldn't separate the calf from Aida. He drank all the milk. Horner's mother was furious.

Once P-40 had succeeded in breaking a fence, he did it with regularity. He went where he wanted, invading the vegetable garden and eating or trampling all the snap beans and squash. Horner, who hated both, was glad and felt that he and P-40 had a special understanding about such things.

But P-40 finally went too far.

Aunt Liz came from Fort Worth in her new Cadillac. It was pale green and beautiful. No one had new cars during the war. There were no tires and gasoline was rationed. But at this time Aunt Liz was married to a wealthy man who had connections in wartime Washington. He once called up to say that Keel was safe, even though his ship had been reported sunk.

Liz drove from Fort Worth for the weekend, and that night the moon was full and bright. Her new Cadillac was parked in the driveway. P-40, apparently curious, came right into the yard by pushing the gate off its hinges.

Everyone in the house was asleep when the first thump came, loud and solid. Horner sat up.

There was a second, louder thump. And this one was followed by a terrible crunch. Horner heard his father getting up, and so he, too, got up and went to the window to look out.

P-40 had butted Aunt Liz's car twice and was backing off to hit it again. There, in the shining new surface of the car, P-40 saw a pale green bull, a reflection in the bright moonlight, angry and ready to charge at him. P-40 put his head down and began pawing the gravel in the driveway. Horner's father let out a yell. P-40 lunged into the car for the third time, this time so hard that he staggered back from the dents he had made in the front fender and door.

Horner's father grabbed a stick of firewood at the back door. He hit P-40 on the rump and hit him again and again until he drove the calf outside the yard.

Aunt Liz stood out in front in her nightgown and wailed about how her beautiful new car had been utterly destroyed by a stupid beast. Horner crept back into bed.

At breakfast the next morning nobody spoke of it until Aunt Liz finally said, "I'm coming back here one of these days, and when I do I want to be served a big, juicy hamburger steak. I want you to tell me, Horner, that I'm having the pleasure of eating that mean cow that wrecked my new car last night."

For the first time since the trip began, Horner found himself alone with Ellie, in a small gallery off the main exhibit room. It housed a single Dubuffet sculpture, placed on a white box in the center of the room. "What does this remind you of?" he asked her.

"A big messy shape with bright paint all over it?"

"You're not trying. If somebody painted graffiti all over the monument on the Lady courthouse lawn it would look like this, wouldn't it?"

"I'm getting nervous. We have to be back by six. We have the party tonight."

"We what?"

"The big party is tonight. I told you all about it. You never listen to me, do you? We've got to change into evening clothes, too."

"Ellie, I'm pooped. I know you won't believe me, but I just can't party anymore this weekend. Why did you agree to this trip if we already had a party tonight? I haven't recovered from last night at Teelee's."

"Well, I thought Mme. deRian would be along—the way she invited us it sounded that way. I was sure that you would get to talk to her and would wind up with a big hunk of the deRian business. You wouldn't be sorry if that had happened, would you?"

Horner showed his disgust by shaking his head. "I thought you were doing this for fun. Is everything business with you?"

"It won't be a complete loss. I've got Father Cranshaw to agree to have dinner with us at the club some evening. His church is

100

the one that all the rich Catholics in Houston attend. I'll make something out of this disaster—just wait and see. Can you imagine having your housekeeper act as hostess?"

Ellie swept back into the main gallery to urge everyone back to the airplane for the trip home.

The moment they were in the air, the stewardess came through with drinks. Horner was seated again beside O'Neal, who now smelled even more rancid than before. Horner noticed that the other priests had picked seats as far away from O'Neal as possible. Horner asked, "Well, how did you like the exhibit?"

O'Neal said, "One Dubuffet is a powerful lot of paint and messing around, isn't it? A whole museum full of them is a bit hard on the old optic system, I would say."

"I'll drink to that."

"You know, it isn't often I get to corner a distinguished lawyer like yourself. I was wondering if you might consider coming out to the university one day and talking to a few of my students?"

Horner smiled. "I work for a distinguished law firm, but I don't think you'd want me on your campus. Do you know that I'm fifty years old, and I think that you're the first priest I've ever spoken to."

"Oh, and a sorry one you had to start with, isn't he? I'm sorry about all the bad jokes this morning."

"No, no—don't be. I just realized this morning when I saw all of you filing into the waiting room that I'm afraid of priests. My mother always said that Catholic priests were agents of the devil because they drink alcohol right in church. There's a little Catholic church in Lady where I grew up, and the priest lived in a house behind it. Sometimes he'd be sitting out on his porch when we'd drive by, and Mama would say, 'I imagine he's drinking himself stupid with one of his cocktails.'"

"And you've seen a bit of evidence today that reinforces your mother's beliefs, eh?" He laughed.

Horner smiled and finished his drink. He clinked the ice cubes. "We used to go on vacation trips to Mexico, and Mama would make us stop and get out of the car and visit every church we came to. She would put a handkerchief on top of her head, and then drag us through, clucking her tongue. Back in the car, we'd get a lecture: 'Did you see all those idols? The Bible clearly says no idols, and that place is full of them. And all that gold up on the ceiling! The Catholic Church just robs the poor people blind to put gold on everything.'"

O'Neal laughed again. "My goodness, you did get an earful, didn't you? It's all true, of course. Your mother would be gratified to know that the church finally has a program now to help the clergy with drinking problems. We tried to ignore it for years, but now we ship 'em off to a hospital and try to dry 'em out." He held up his empty glass in a signal.

The stewardess came immediately. She said, "Now, you two gentlemen are men after my own heart. The pilot says we've run into a heavy head wind, and it's going to take us an hour or so longer than it should to get back to Houston. We've got a whole case of Scotch on board, and I'm hoping you'll drink it all up. I don't want to have to carry it off the plane." She kept their glasses full after that.

O'Neal said, "As for the decorated churches in Mexico, it seems to me that every country gets the Catholic churches it needs. What do you think about the churches in this country?"

"I don't really know anything about them. I shouldn't even talk about this subject. I don't think I've ever been inside one. . . ."

By the time Ellie came back to tell Horner that she had discovered they were going to be even later getting back to Houston, Horner and O'Neal were drunk. Ellie took Horner's glass away from him. "Not one more drop!" she scolded.

O'Neal blinked in surprise at her vehemence. When she was out of earshot, he leaned over and said to Horner, "I feel pretty much about women the way you do about us priests." He burst out laughing and his face turned an astonishing mixture of purple and scarlet.

After he finished his laughing fit, O'Neal hiccupped and said, "Oh, excuse me."

"Is it okay if I ask you a question?" Horner asked.

"Priests and prostitutes," O'Neal said.

"What?"

"That's what everyone always wants to know about priests and about prostitutes—how did you get to be one?"

"That's right! Why did you decide to become a priest? I wanted to ask you that."

"My mother, God bless her soul. She told me to."

"Just like that?"

O'Neal nodded solemnly. Horner decided he looked like Oliver Hardy without the little Hitler mustache.

Horner said, "My mother wanted me to become a Methodist minister, but I believe that you have to be called to the ministry."

"Called?"

"God would have said something like, 'Okay, Horner Bonner, quit fooling around in law school. I want you to become a Methodist preacher.' I kept thinking maybe he would say something like that to me, but he never did."

"You believe that He calls some people? Talks to them in a deep voice like that?"

"Some people say He calls them, and that's what I believed when I was younger."

O'Neal sipped his drink and thought it over. "Well, I guess I'll drink to that," he said, blinking.

Ellie insisted on driving home from the airport, although Horner thought probably he was sober enough. True, he couldn't remember how many drinks he had had, but he really felt better now than he had earlier in the day.

"My God," Ellie said, "but you are a hypocrite!"

"Oh?"

"All these years you and your mother have been going around saying ugly things about the Catholic Church and then you and that fat priest wind up thick as thieves."

"I never called him 'Father,' and you and that professional cocktail piano man were practically into love duets or something shocking—right there in front of a dozen other priests and your own husband. It was, 'Oh, Father, you play so divinely,' and 'Oh,

Father, tell me this,' and 'Oh, Father, tell me that!' It looked as if you were getting a case of the hots."

"The man is gay! Can't you tell a gay when you see one, Horner? I don't mean he's out picking up boys. I think he's probably celibate or whatever it is that priests are supposed to be. I was just getting his be-nice-to-the-middle-aged-lady treatment. He's an expert at it."

"That's funny You don't look middle-aged." He patted her on the arm.

She laughed. "Don't tell me you're going to get all amorous on me, right here on the freeway. When we get home, we've got to get dressed and get back to town. I'll call and tell Phyllis that we're running late."

In his alcoholic haze, Horner suddenly thought of Joyce-Joy Nelson and the night they drove out Whiteland Hill Road where everyone parks. He was sixteen. He felt unaccountably hot. They necked. His skin burned. He got the zipper on the side of her dress open.

"You are so hot," she breathed.

"It's you . . ." Horner said, "you're making me hot."

Joyce-Joy had red hair, and she was famous among the boys in high school for her shapely behind. She also played the piano, made good grades and was a nice girl.

Nice meant that she pretended she didn't feel his throbbing prick pressed against her thigh, and she wouldn't let him get his hand up between her legs. But they French kissed with abandon. He worked her bra off one breast, with no help from her, and touched the rough tip of her nipple with a fingertip, gently, until she let out a little moan. The sound embarrassed her. She pulled herself together and insisted he take her home.

Horner's balls ached. He was burning hot and dizzy. He'd never felt quite like this after a necking session before, and he told Joyce-Joy as much. He decided this was real love.

"You really were hot tonight, Horner," she agreed at her door.

The next day he broke out with measles and was miserably sick for two weeks. But by the time he got back to school Joyce-Joy was going steady with a skinny guy who played two-piano duets with her. Their version of "That Old Black Magic" was the sensation of the spring assembly. Everyone agreed that they ought to become professionals and go play piano in a Dallas nightclub.

As they walked through the kitchen, Ellie put on a pot of coffee. "Get in the shower. I'll bring you a cup as soon as it's ready."

Horner was sobering up fast, thanks to the ride on the freeway with Ellie at the wheel. Her driving always frightened him, but he wasn't allowed to comment on her speeding or on the way she passed cars on the wrong side.

The clock on the dresser in the bedroom said seven thirty. It felt like midnight. Horner longed to crawl into the big bed and snuggle down under the yellow puff. Instead, he undressed and went dutifully into his bathroom. He would get into the shower and get the water adjusted. Then Ellie would go into her bathroom and start the water for her tub and steal off all his hot water. While he was thinking about this problem, it happened. He held his head under the cold spray for a minute and then shut it off.

She came in with his coffee. "Oh, you got your hair wet, Horner! Now you'll look like a slicked-down rat. Why don't you use my hair dryer?"

"Go tend to your bathwater, Ellie. You'll be flooding us out."

"I forgot!" She fled.

He rubbed his hair with a towel, a big, soft, dark brown towel with an EHB monogram. Ellie had her initials on everything in the house.

He checked his eyeballs in the mirror. Not too bad. He took a sip of coffee and appraised his features. Everyone had always told him he looked like Keel. They had both had blond hair as little boys, but Horner's had become dark brown and now it was getting gray. Keel's had stayed blond and Horner wondered if he bleached it. The coffee was hot, but weak. Ellie couldn't make coffee worth a damn. Since the children had left, she had all but given up cooking. He made the morning coffee and left it on the warmer for her. She went to her tennis club for lunch. In the evening they either went out or just had Post Toasties with skimmed milk. They had both become quite thin, and all their friends were jealous. Horner, however, found that he was hungry all the time. He wondered if maybe the reason he seemed to be drinking more might not be because he was hungry.

He managed to get a couple of drops of Visine in each eye, although by the time he finished half the coffee, his hands were shaking.

He had never learned how to tie a bow tie so Ellie had to do it for him and help with his studs, too. He hated evening clothes. What business did a boy who grew up in Lady have pretending he was important enough to wear such an elitist costume? The girl at the party last night had called his family snobs. Was he a snob?

"Ah, but you look just beautiful, baby," Ellie said. She always said that to stop him from complaining about the whole business of evening clothes.

"I don't know why we have to do this at the club. Is it the president's anniversary party or something?"

"We're not going to our club, baby. Didn't you understand? We're going to the Petrol Club. I told you all about it last week."

"The Petrol Club! Jesus, Ellie, I hate that place. Don't you know that Taylow or one of the other partners could be there? It's Saturday night, and they hang out there."

"Phyllis Jones invited us. We're at their table."

"I'm sick. I'm going to be sicker."

"Mrs. Taylow likes you, Horner! Are you going to pretend you don't remember that I told you all about this invitation?"

"I swear to you I don't remember a word! I must have been drunk. I would have put my foot down. We don't belong in that crowd, Ellie. I don't enjoy drinking when I'm around them. I'm afraid I'll say something I'll regret later. Couldn't we just have a quiet weekend one time? I'm worn out! You're going to have to ship me off to dry out pretty soon or else I'm going to be back in the hospital with my ulcer bleeding again."

"Threats, threats. You look splendid, baby. Never better. Now zip me up and let's go. You understand now why I didn't want us to be late?"

In the car, Horner said, "This is one of your plots, isn't it, Ellie? I can read you. I know what you're up to."

"You just leave everything to me."

"Little Rock was one of your specials, wasn't it? You thought we were going to charm the deRians and wow the Rockefellers." He laughed. "I hope you found your gay priest and the Dubuffets entertaining—if not profitable. My priest had the worst funk I've smelled since Lady High's locker room."

"Don't talk, baby. Your voice sounds tired. Just tend to your driving and get us there in one piece. I'll take care of everything."

By the time they got off the elevator at the top of Houston's tallest bank building, Horner's black Italian slippers had begun to hurt his feet. They entered the huge room with its chandeliers made of old wagon wheels and its murals of brown cactus. Horner spotted the Joneses' table. His heart sank. Mr. and Mrs. Taylow were there, too—the old man himself. Had Ellie known and kept it from him?

Mrs. Taylow had her face turned up before Horner even reached her, demanding the kiss on the cheek she always got from the junior members of the firm. Ellie was hugged by Taylow and by Jones and Evans in turn. Their wives smiled greetings and made little noises.

Ellie said, "I'm so sorry we're late. The deRian plane ran into this head wind on the way back from Winrock or we'd have been back in plenty of time."

Horner watched the other women's faces as Ellie dropped the names. They were impressed. Ellie would make it pay.

Mrs. Taylow said, "Oh, Horner, how exciting! I want to hear all about the ranch at Winrock. I've heard they have this fabulous breeding program. . . ."

People were shuffled at the table so Horner could sit next to Mrs. Taylow. She would want all the details about the artificial insemination project, Horner knew.

But before he could even start, Taylow was on his feet and holding out his glass. "I don't see why we should delay any longer. Horner, we're having this little dinner for you tonight to let you know we've decided to make you a partner. Oh, we won't be putting Bonner in the firm's name right away. Taylow, Jones, Evans and Erbowski is too well established to go tinkering with, but now you're going to be a full partner in every other way—the youngest the firm has had since Evans here was elevated almost twenty years ago. We need some new young blood, and we think that, in addition to handling our real-estate department, you're ready now to help the rest of us bring in some major new clients. I don't mind saying that a little business from deRians and Rockefellers would be most welcome. . . ."

"Hear, hear!" Jones said. He was a former governor of Texas, and his political connections were supposed to be a key factor in the firm's success. He had had only one spectacularly bad term in office, elected because voters confused him in the Democratic primary with another Jones. He was already drunk.

Evans said, "Let's drink to Horner and Ellie and welcome them aboard the captain's bridge." He talked that way because he had once been a commander in the navy.

The men stood and drank.

Horner knew that his face was burning. He decided that Taylow had heard that he had been talking to Ollie Oil. Ollie was looking for a lawyer to put in charge of their leasing division so Taylow was heading him off. Horner hoped his too-long pause, his obvious confusion, would be taken as modesty and surprise. Finally he said, "Ellie, were you in on this?"

They all laughed. Ellie looked down. "When Phyllis told me the Taylows were going to be here tonight, I did sort of hope . . . That's why I didn't mention them to you, Horner."

"Well, if I seem at a loss for words, it's because I am." Horner thought, What a dumb thing to say. "I hadn't the slightest idea a partnership was in the offing. I'm not at all sure that I'll be any great asset when it comes to bringing in new business—that will have to be Ellie's job. And I'll see that she works at it, too."

They all laughed and toasted Ellie.

The orchestra began to play. Horner leaned down and asked Mrs. Taylow to dance. Her diamonds looked very bright against the white powder of her withered neck.

She said, "I hope we're going to hustle, Horner. Jay Jay won't even try, he's such an old stick in the mud."

Horner was afraid he detected a new familiarity. Would he have to call Taylow "Jay Jay"?

The orchestra was playing "Red Roses for a Blue Lady." He and Ellie did the same uncomplicated box step they had done the first time they danced almost thirty years earlier. On the dance floor with Ellie he didn't have to worry about saying something that would offend someone at their illustrious table.

"I'm tired, Ellie," he whispered in her ear.

"It's been a long day. Ease up on the booze now, will you, honey?"

The orchestra shifted into "The Yellow Rose of Texas," but kept it slow. "Promise me one thing."

"Hummm?"

"Promise me that you won't plan a single goddamn thing for next weekend, will you?"

"You'll have to tell your mother we aren't coming, then. She's counting on it."

"Counting on what?"

"You don't remember anything, do you? Keel is coming up from La Isla and Flannel will be down from New York. Your mother expects all you boys to show up for some kind of recital that Banyan is playing at the university on Friday night, and then you'll do your reunioning all day Saturday. I told her of course you and I wouldn't miss it for the world."

Horner sobbed softly in her ear, a fake bid for sympathy. "Last time we all got together—it must have been more than ten years ago, don't you remember? It's depressing for me to have to see where I'm going to be twenty years from now. And there is all that tension between Keel and Field. . . . My stomach aches just remembering it. And Flannel might as well have a string of big worry beads to click. . . . I never have been able to figure out what that bunch expects of me."

❋   ❋   ❋

In the car on the way home, Ellie began stroking the back of his neck. Her bracelets jangled. Horner felt his fatigue returning with a rush. "What if I say no?" he asked.

"No? You've never said no in thirty years. Why would you start tonight?"

"I'm not talking about sex. I'm talking about the new job."

"Oh, don't be a horse's ass. Of course, you'll take it." She pulled away, over to her side of the front seat.

"Did you hear what they expect? It's like working for a big corporation and then getting named to the board. You think, Wheee, I'm on the inside so I'll know what's going on at the top. But what's going on at the top is just more worrying than goes on at the lower levels. I can barely keep up with what I'm supposed to do now, Ellie. Did you hear Jay Jay? They expect me to come up with new business for the other divisions, too. Did you know they keep a list of such things and run a check every three months on everyone in the firm? I usually come out okay as head of real estate. As a partner I'm going to be low man on the totem pole. Remember Hal? He was a partner, and he's gone, disappeared."

"You said he got a better job with Monsanto."

"Oh, I don't expect you to understand what goes on inside a law firm, but I specialized too soon. I haven't done anything but real estate for so long I can't even consult intelligently on any of the rest of it. I'm lucky because Houston has boomed, but I'm in the right spot right now. If I try to grab hold of some big case outside of a simple title contract dispute, God help me!"

"Oh, hush up, Horner. You're just running off at the mouth. You're nothing but a worrier—just like your mother. You'll see. You're just tired tonight. Tomorrow it will all look better. And if you want your name in the firm's title, I'm sure we can manage that. This is going to be wonderful. I can hardly wait to tell Teelee! Gordon will print your picture in the paper and everything!"

Horner tried to read through the Sunday paper while he drank his coffee. He couldn't focus on any story more than a few seconds. His mind kept going back to the scene at the club last night, to his new job and what it would mean.

Ellie didn't stir when he went back into the bedroom to get his shaving gear, an overnight bag and a few clothes. He pulled on the old cotton pants he wore when he mowed the lawn.

It took a few minutes to find a pencil stub in the kitchen and there was no paper at all. He tore the side off a Post Toasties box and wrote on the gray inside:

"Dear Ellie—I've gone to the ranch for a day or two—or maybe more. Please call Lottie first thing in the morning and tell her I won't be in. She'll tell Taylow's secretary. Love, Horner."

It felt odd, writing a note to Ellie. Horner realized that they had not been apart in years—not even for a single night. And yet she was a stranger. Had she always been so ambitious for him? Was it just her age?

He pulled on an old flannel shirt, picked up his bag and went out to the car. Just the gesture of tossing his bag into the backseat seemed to ease the tension a little.

He backed the car out of the long driveway and checked his watch. It was almost seven, and the sun would pop above the horizon at any moment. The day was already bright.

Horner didn't stop in Austin but bypassed it on the superhighway. If he had stopped he would have felt obliged to call Banyan and explain why he was going to Lady, when he really couldn't even explain it to himself.

West of Austin were the familiar beige hills with scrub cedar and beautiful pale rocks. Occasionally he would see five or six goats or a dozen Herefords, a stone house with a windmill and tank, three or four new cars and pickup trucks parked in a driveway. Sometimes there were entrances along the highway, often elaborate, with the ranch name—Rancho Grande or Timon's Acres—arched above the cattle guard. Beyond, out of sight of the highway, would be the rambling ranch house, sometimes with tennis court and swimming pool, a working ranch owned by some Houston doctor who used it as a tax shelter and a lavish weekend retreat, a fantasy of the Old West for some former New Yorker. Horner had handled the papers on these deals.

Horner told himself that he had no illusions about real ranch life. It was a terrible, hard, mean, cruel way to try to survive. During the war his father hadn't been able to hire any help, so the two of them had tried to look after everything. There was too much land, poor land, and too many cattle to care for properly. So many died, of hookworm and other diseases—mostly because Horner didn't find them until it was too late to get the vet.

Horner had hated those years. And long after, the dying animals, the loss in money that each death meant, haunted him. His own children had loved visiting the ranch when they were little. They couldn't understand why he said he didn't want to live on a ranch. He would tell them he couldn't face the sight of a cow with maggots feeding in the holes in her ears; a ewe, wool caught in a barbed-wire fence, dead; chickens killed by a mad skunk, wantonly; tiny pigs eaten by their parents because Horner hadn't gotten them out of the pen quickly enough. And then P-40 and all the other beautiful, life-loving calves, his pets, turned into hamburger that stuck in his throat when he tried to swallow.

Horner didn't recognize the man who was working at the 7-Eleven store, but then almost everyone in Lady was a stranger to him now. He'd been gone almost thirty years, after all. Horner got eggs and bacon, bread, coffee and beans—camper's grub. It might be cool enough so that the eggs and bacon would be okay for a couple of days.

The Eden highway had a new surface since he had last been out. A couple of years earlier, he had come for a weekend of bird shooting and serious drinking. Horner had been uncomfortable somehow with all the booze and partying at what he thought of as his mother's house. When the friends hinted again this fall that it would be fun to repeat the outing, Horner said he guessed not. Ellie was annoyed. The women had come along just for the partying—none of them would shoot a bird. They played bridge almost nonstop for two days. On Sunday afternoon, Field sent out an old man named Cha-Cha to barbecue the doves over a pit.

112

They had shot more than a hundred birds, and the flavor, the way Cha-Cha cooked them in his special sauce, was unforgettable.

The ranch was eighteen miles from Lady. Horner had driven it about a jillion times in to Lady High—even during the war years there had been gas for school. He had been too young for the war and by the time Korea came along, he was married and he and Ellie had a baby. Horner wondered if he might be different if he had gone into the army. Flannel was the only one of the brothers who seemed to have been markedly changed by his experience. Flannel hadn't expected to be drafted because he was so skinny. But he was pulled right out of the university, zip, and sent to boot camp. When he came home at the end of the war he cursed a blue streak, smoked cigarettes and had a kind of indifference, a screen around himself, that Horner hadn't remembered. It had seemed an unpleasant act at first, a veneer that Flannel had tried on and then decided to keep. In thinking about it, Horner decided that most of the people he knew from New York had that same kind of hard surface. That's probably why Flannel was right at home in New York, why he would never come back to Texas to live.

Horner was tired. He flexed the muscles in his back and speeded up. He had been driving for more than five hours. It was almost three when he turned off the highway, rattled across the pipes of the cattle guard and knew that he had only two more miles. The road, seldom traveled now, was little more than a couple of ruts and dead weeds. He had to slow down or risk the chance of knocking a hole in something on the bottom of the car.

He came over the slight hill and everything looked the same as he remembered. The house was of stones that the workmen had gathered nearby, mostly from the dry creek bed not more than seventy-five feet from the house site. Everything else was the brown of early spring, too.

The house was a rectangular box, two stories high, with a tin roof and a screened porch across the front. In summer they had eaten out on the porch, and when the nights were hot the boys slept out there. The porch was on the east, overlooking the tank.

113

The tank had started out as a kind of natural low place, one that often retained water for a week or so after a rain—longer than any other spot for miles around. After the war, with federal money and an expert who came with the heavy equipment, the land above the spot was dug out and the hard clay was moved around to build a dam across the runoff spot. The tank became a pond that never went completely dry no matter how long the rainless spells.

At first sight, it was a big blue mirror reflecting the few clouds in the intense March sky. But Horner knew that up close the water was a mucky brown, surrounded by smelly cow flops and thirsty snakes among the burr-covered weeds.

This water hole was the reason that Moser next door leased the whole Bonner ranch for his cattle. This single little mudhole helped make all the worthless land around it valuable. When there was rain, that land would come alive with grass, and for a year or two it could feed a few hundred cows.

There had been too little rain this past winter and fall, however, and now it was all bare and brown, a kind of dusty stubble between the rocks. And the scene filled Horner with the old dismay.

He left the motor running while he got out to unlock the gate and drive through. He shut the gate but didn't bother to lock it. It had never been locked during all the years they lived out here. He parked in back of the house under the big live oak that had lost half its top in a tornado. That same wind had lifted up part of the roof and then dropped it back into place with a terrifying crash. The windows were sucked out of their frames, and the quilt on Horner's bed had been sucked up against the window screens in his room. Horner's father had come to the door. "Are you all right?"

"What was that crash?"

"Tornado just blew over. I think we're okay, though."

They were okay, but the big oak had been deformed ever since. His mother's chicken house, with all her laying hens and new chicks inside, had just disappeared from the face of the earth. Horner said, "The angels in heaven are going to be eating my fried chicken every Sunday now instead of me." His mother

114

quoted him at church and all around until he wished he'd never said it.

He carried his paper bag of groceries in one arm, fished out the key from a half-buried tin can and unlocked the back door. It was a familiar feeling, bringing something in from the car. The windows on the back of the house were boarded over with plywood that had been cut to fit. He would pull off the one in the kitchen to get some light in there. The windows on the front were protected by the screened porch.

The smell inside was of dust and dryness. It was warm because the sun had baked the stones all day. Horner liked the warmth. There would be a bit of cold in the air as soon as the sun was gone.

He put his groceries on the cabinet. There was a hammer in the kitchen closet, just where it had always been. He went out and pulled off the plywood window and flooded the kitchen with golden afternoon sun.

He made the rounds of all the rooms, opened the front door and walked around the porch where the old bridge table with four kitchen chairs still sat. Upstairs he took one of the canvas cots and brought it down to the living room. He would sleep there and cook in the fireplace. He went out back and gathered up some dried sticks and boards from the cow lot fences and sheds that had fallen into ruin years ago. It was depressing. He had wanted a sense of coming home, but his mother had taken all her furniture to her house in town. There was nothing homelike about it.

He arranged the wood in the fireplace, put candles and matches on the mantel and went back upstairs to the hall closet for a quilt. The light was dim, but when he pulled off the top quilt he heard the soft, paperlike rustle that made him shiver. Under the quilt was a dry snakeskin, intact. His mother would love to hear that the old snake still was coming back to shed its skin in the same place. Year after year the skin had turned up in this closet. No one ever knew how the snake got into the house. No one had ever seen it. Horner thought, I want to shed something like skin. . . .

On the stairs he shook out the quilt to make sure there were no scorpions in it. It was faded, made of old feed sacks. His mother had made several such quilts for the boys' camping trips. The batting was held in place by knotted strings rather than fine quilting. But these covers had endured. They had served as play places for babies on the floor and as mattresses for the boys when too many relatives came to visit and took over the beds.

Horner sat on the cot and pulled off his shoes. It was only five thirty in the afternoon, but he was tired. He put his watch inside one of his shoes, pulled the quilt up and let the sagging canvas cradle him.

He had an odd feeling, for just an instant before he fell asleep, that his father was upstairs and therefore everything was perfectly fine. He hadn't felt that way in years.

FOUR

Banyan Bonner

BANYAN Bonner unlocked the door to the music building and let himself in. Practice rooms were on the third floor. He walked up without stopping off by his office. He would do his warm-ups this morning and then get in a last, serious practice session later.

He turned on the lights in the tiny room that was filled almost completely with an old Steinway concert grand, battered and crazed with fine white webbing. Some child or midget must have been in here before him—he had to spin down the old-fashioned, round-seated stool.

He sat, rubbed his hands together and listened for a moment to the absolute silence of the building. This was his favorite time of day. It belonged to him. It was the last time the building would be quiet until late tonight.

He began the day's noise with a scale in C major, both hands, fingers moving up one note at a time, measured, clearly now . . . up, up, three octaves, not too fast . . . Now, shift up a note. Make each sound round, complete. Stately—slow down. It's running away this morning. Slower. His mother and brother Flannel were coming this afternoon. He hadn't seen Flannel since their father's funeral nine years ago.

At some point his fingers and all the years of practice took over entirely. Banyan's mind slipped free. It always did when he did warm-ups.

119

The first scales of the day were home base. Everything started there. He was part of a recital tonight in the hall downstairs, a faculty thing. He was to open the program with his Chopin, and then he would be accompanying the department's star of the moment, a young French flute player who thought he was better than Rampal and who was playing Telemann's Sonata in F minor and the Poulenc Sonata that was a Rampal specialty. Banyan detested the young man. But over the years he had come to understand that he would always hate the new star.

The practice room was roaring with Banyan's scales. Waves of rich noise engulfed him. Three octaves up, three down. He muttered to himself the way he spoke to his students. Is that left hand trailing a bit? Up, up, up . . . Mrs. Sitton's voice often was still there, mixed with the scales. And sometimes he heard Mad Marshall d'Bose. Every teacher he had ever had talked to him as he practiced.

In 1932, Paderewski made a farewell concert tour that took him to San Antonio. Banyan was twelve. Mrs. Sitton drove five of her pupils the hundred and sixty miles from Lady to hear the great man play. Banyan returned in a state of exaltation.

He had to tell his mother about it and Flannel was there. Horner, who had chronic ear problems, was crying softly against their mother's leg. "Memorial Hall is an old barn. The orchestra won't play there, Mrs. Sitton says, but it's the only place big enough for the crowds." Banyan's eyes were lit from his excitement. "It was packed. We were about in the middle, to one side, and the piano was bigger than any piano in Lady—a concert grand, Mrs. Sitton says, made in Germany especially for Paderewski. It would take up half our living room. The piano was sitting there out in front of these old purple curtains.

"Finally a man came out and fiddled with the bench, got it just the right height, and then everybody got absolutely quiet.

"Then this old, old man came out." Banyan stopped and acted out the moment. "I mean he is old—older than Miss McGorey at church. He walks out slow, creeping out from behind the curtains, and he's holding onto the piano so he won't fall down. The people jump up and everybody claps. He sits down slowly on his bench. He has white hair, and it's long and bushy. He rests there for a minute. Then slowly he lifts up his hands, holds them above the keys for a minute and then, blam! It's just unbelievable! This skinny little old man who looks feeble as hell rips into—!"

"Banyan!" Their mother was startled by the hell. But clearly her interruption came only from habit. She was caught up, too, in Banyan's description.

Banyan continued: "He was scarcely moving at all except for his hands, and the music was just pouring out over us, big music, a roar of music. When he finished the first piece everyone jumped up screaming and clapping, and Mrs. Sitton was crying."

Flannel said, "She cries when *you* play! You're always saying you can make her cry just by putting a little juice in the Schubert."

"Shut up, Flannel," Banyan said.

Their mother said, "Stop it, boys."

Banyan said, "After the concert was over he had to hold onto the piano lid to stand up, and then he shuffled off behind the curtains, and we all just stood there and clapped and yelled and Mrs. Sitton blew her nose and smeared her rouge. She didn't say a word the whole drive back home, if you can believe it."

Just as scales always conjured up Mrs. Sitton's nervous, frail voice and trembling hands, Bach invariably brought to mind Dr. d'Bose. He had been head of the university's music department when Banyan, at seventeen, first arrived in Austin. The music building, just to the west of the leaping horses fountain, was new then. Dr. d'Bose had studied in Germany. He knew every Bach prelude and fugue for the organ from memory. He had perfect pitch.

Banyan went to the concert hall to start his lesson at the exact time it was scheduled. Often he followed a blind girl who was brought to her organ lesson by a nun. The girl would hear Banyan's first step onto the stage, and she would stop, turn stiffly and let herself off the bench abruptly. She just broke off whatever she was playing, often leaving chords hanging unresolved in the air. It was unsettling.

"Hi. How ya doin'?" Banyan said cheerfully.

She said, "He didn't like my Mendelssohn today. The sixth sonata." She was plump and took vague, tiny steps, impatient for her seeing-eye nun to come up on the stage for her.

"Did he tell you that?"

"He didn't have to. I could tell. . . ." The nun frowned at him, touched the girl's arm and led her away.

Banyan was afraid of nuns.

The stage was paneled in golden woods and brightly lit. Stainless-steel pipes were on each side and across the back. Dr. d'Bose had had the organ designed and built in Germany.

Banyan slipped off his loafers, climbed onto the bench and pushed in all the stops the blind girl had left out. He opened his music, set the stops and began to play.

At some point, Dr. d'Bose would come in the back of the hall and take a seat. Banyan never heard him enter. Usually it was a wrong note that sent d'Bose into action. His perfect pitch had been painfully pricked. "No, no!" he cried out, startling Banyan, who often was well into a distracted daze if the piece was something he had almost memorized. "It's A sharp, not B! Can't you hear the way the line is moving up in the left hand? And I think you missed an E with your foot about six measures back. . . ."

If he were full of energy, Dr. d'Bose might come up and push Banyan over on the bench and play the passage that Banyan had botched. Dr. d'Bose was a tall, thin, dry man. He never praised anything that Banyan ever did at the organ, but he never quite gave up on him either. The fact that Banyan remained one of Dr. d'Bose's students throughout four years at the university was unique. Dr. d'Bose had a reputation for getting bored with students quickly, and since he was in charge of the music school he could easily shift a disappointing student into some other teacher's care.

At the end of his junior year, just before he went out on the stage to play his finals, Banyan had to go outside the music building. From sheer nervousness, he threw up all over one of the gardenia bushes. Later he would use his terrible, unpredictable nervousness as an excuse, to himself, to explain why he never had been quite able to make it as a concert performer. He was drafted into the army after his four years at the university and spent almost another four years during the war standing guard duty, washing dishes in an army hospital in California, and then giving tests to new recruits in an army base in Louisiana.

After his discharge, Banyan used the GI bill to get a master's degree at Juilliard in New York. He was an outsider there. It took him three years. He always blamed the army years during which he never played either organ or piano. His technique never seemed to have the ease he had known before the war. He said that the interruption had destroyed his chances for a serious career. But to himself he came to understand that he simply wasn't good enough, nor tough enough, nor steady enough. His playing was erratic. Dr. d'Bose was gracious about hiring him after he sort of faded from Juilliard. His master's recital had been reviewed by a third-string critic from *The New York Times*. His Bach had been found "indecisive." Banyan always wondered if he had played Chopin instead of Bach that evening, would his whole life have been different?

After a few arpeggios Banyan shifted into a Bach prelude and lost himself almost instantly. He tried to hold the rhythm fixed. It was almost impossible now that he was past fifty to memorize any new music, but a few things he had learned early were in his fingers, programmed there like the scales. If he thought about the notes, the key he was playing in, the time, nothing would come. But if he just started it, the whole composition might come rattling out with no effort on his part. The process was wonderfully automatic. It was like being in a trance, hypnotized. Or, depending on the music, it could be like being possessed.

He always felt, however, that he performed better when the music was newly learned, when every part of his consciousness was turned on, to feeling through the musical lines.

This particular Bach prelude always made him think of one of his mother's quilts, put together with tiny, regular diamond shapes and squares that formed a larger square of four parts until the bright colors and the even stitches that held it together were a big bedspread of astonishing beauty that dazzled the senses.

There was a banging on the door to the practice room. Banyan realized that the pounding had been going on for some time and was growing louder and more impatient.

He broke off, irritated that the vision of the quilt was gone, that the singing voices had been halted. The door banging was Mrs. Leary's unsubtle touch. He leaned around and opened the door. "It wasn't locked. I never lock it, Mrs. Leary."

"Good morning! Good morning, Mr. Bonner! Our little Elliott is here, and he's got this room signed up for the next hour, haven't we, Elliott?"

Elliott looked at the floor in embarrassment. "I'm really sorry, Mr. Bonner, but I have a lesson at nine and Mrs. Dryfuss will kill me if I fumble through this damn Handel again."

Banyan said, "It's all right, Elliott. I've got to be on my way. I have our favorite old lady all warmed up for you."

Banyan and all the other faculty members were aware that Elliott at eighteen was a better pianist than any of them. Even as a child he had been. He probably could have a career as a performer if he could overcome some of his pitiful shyness.

Mrs. Leary was back at her desk where she ruled the third-floor practice rooms. Students signed up for their hours and heaven help them if they didn't show up as scheduled. For her favorites, Mrs. Leary could always find a room. But Mrs. Leary did not like homosexuals, and they had a difficult time of it on Mrs. Leary's third floor.

Mrs. Leary gave every male music student a test of her own devising, one that Banyan never forgot. Mrs. Leary had been in charge of the third floor even back in the days when he was a new arrival. She loved to gossip with the students. Shortly after he enrolled in the music department, Banyan was sitting on the edge of her desk, waiting for the hour so he could take over a practice room.

Suddenly there was a sharp, piercing pain in one of his buttocks. He jumped up and turned to see that Mrs. Leary had just stuck him with a pin, an old-fashioned hat pin.

"What the hell was that for?" he said angrily.

Mrs. Leary smiled sweetly up at him, pleased. "Now, now, it's all right. I just wanted to find out if you was a fairy. I give all the pretty young boys my fairy test. If you had jumped up and squealed like a girl, I'd have known you was a fairy."

Banyan never sat on her desk in the hallway again and never gossiped with her either. But after the test, Mrs. Leary always considered him one of "me lads." She was thrilled when he came back from Juilliard to join the faculty, and he was the only teacher she would go to hear perform. "He plays like an angel, he does," she would say about him to students and to others on the faculty.

So Mrs. Leary was referred to as "Banyan's groupie" or the president of Banyan's Fan Club of one. Sometimes after she praised his playing she would add in a hissed whisper, "And he's not a fairy either."

Banyan's first student of the day was a freshman, Harriet Faye Franklin. She had a crush on him. He did his best to ignore such complications and conducted the lessons from behind his desk while she sat at the piano.

She was waiting in the hall outside his office as he took out his keys. "Good morning, Harriet," he said.

"I heard you up on the third floor, Mr. Bonner. Why do you practice up there when you have a piano in your studio?"

"Habit. I like that old Steinway especially. It used to be in the concert hall when I was a student here. It knows my fingers. And the sound in a practice room just swallows up my brains." He unlocked his door and stepped back to let Harriet go in ahead of him.

Then Banyan nodded to Dorothea Draga, the voice teacher who had her studio next door. "Morning, Dottie," he said as she unlocked her door.

At that same moment, Harriet, just inside his doorway, strangled over some kind of scream and dropped her sheet music and handbag. She whirled and grabbed at Banyan, clutching him and pushing her face into his chest. He quickly pushed her aside so he could see and moved past her into his studio. There on the floor was a long body sprawled in an impossible contortion. One arm was twisted up on the piano bench. The body in dirty blue jeans was so skinny it could be no one but J. W. Hopkins, one of Banyan's students.

And there was blood, dark and matted on the bench and on the floor.

Dottie looked in the door. "Oh, my God! He's nailed his hand to the bench!" She made it sound like a poor translation of an Italian opera.

Banyan was unfrozen by the thought of opera, of the melodrama. Dottie turned it into a bit of melodrama. He knelt and put a hand to J.W.'s throat. "He's alive. Call the switchboard and tell her to get a doctor and an ambulance here."

A couple of other students had heard Harriet's scream and they pushed past her to look in. "Holy shit!" one said.

Banyan yelled, "Get out! Close the door!"

Dottie said into the phone, "It's an emergency. A student has been injured. There's blood! Yes, it's serious. He's unconscious. Get a doctor! Do whatever you do in emergencies! He's in Bonner's office." She hung up. "That woman is stupid!"

J.W. clearly had taken a nail and driven it through the palm of his left hand, pinning himself to the piano bench. He had used a French bronze weight from Banyan's desk as a hammer. Then, apparently, J.W. had fainted and fallen into this grotesque position. "Help me move him around, Dottie."

"God, Banyan . . . I don't think you're supposed to move a body when it's injured, are you?"

Banyan cursed under his breath and by pulling on J.W.'s sneakered foot got one of his twisted legs straightened. Banyan looked around for something to remove the nail. He needed a hammer. He left J.W. and opened the door where several students were milling around. Harriet was there, white-faced, leaning against the wall, clutching her music. "Here, Harriet," Banyan said, "give me your music. Go find Alex, will you? He's usually in the basement. Tell him to bring a claw hammer right away."

Harriet said, "J.W. drove a nail through his hand, didn't he? That's what I saw. . . ." The students around her gasped in chorus.

Banyan said, "Go on. Hurry! The doctor will be here in a few minutes, I hope. But he won't have a hammer with him."

Banyan said to the other students, "Okay, go on to your classes. Help's on the way, kids."

Back in his office, Dottie was watching anxiously out the window. Banyan put Harriet's music on his desk and went back to kneel again by J.W. He lifted the torso so it wasn't so slumped and twisted. Time seemed to freeze. It was an eternity since he had first unlocked his door. Banyan watched the small pulse beat steadily in J.W.'s Adam's apple. What an utter, stupid fool. A freaked-out, fucked-up kid.

Dottie finally said, "Oh! Here's the doctor! I'll go meet him! Show him the way!" She rushed out just as Alex, a sad black man in overalls, arrived with a hammer, his pliers, a screwdriver and shears.

Alex took one look and his eyes rolled up in his head. "Good Godalmighty! What has that boy gone and done to himself!"

Banyan said, "The doctor's on his way in. Just wait until he tells us what to do."

Alex now was fascinated. "Did this boy think he's going to be Jesus Christ? These music students of yours, Mr. Bonner, they are the craziest. I used to think the physics students was the craziest when I had that building over there, but none of them never come close to trying anything like this. . . . Whooo . . ."

The doctor, a young intern from University Hospital's emergency room, came in. He stood for a moment, taking in the odd scene, a pietà with Banyan as Mary. "Well, this is a new one. . . ."

He knelt on the other side of J.W. and checked the pulse. He turned to Alex. "Let me have the pliers." Dottie, who had followed the doctor in after showing him the way, gave a small operatic cry and ran from the room, heels clicking on the floor.

The doctor got out a large wad of cotton and poured disinfectant into it. He put it on J.W.'s hand beside the nail. Then he took the pliers and pulled at the nail. It came out easily. He said, "The boy passed out before he could pound it into the wood too far." He quickly worked over the wound. "Let's get him out to my car. The ambulance boys may be ten or fifteen minutes behind me—

they were at the coffee shop when your call came. I want to get him into a hospital bed."

The doctor lifted J.W. on one side and Banyan took the other. They arranged his arms over their shoulders, but his feet dragged clumsily, his head sagged down onto his chest. The doctor said, "I don't think we'll hurt him. Let's go."

Alex said, "I'll clean up all this. . . ."

Banyan grunted. "Get that bench out of my office, will you? Bring me a stool or a chair—anything."

"Yes, sir. I'll take care of it."

The doctor's small Ford was at the front entrance. Several students watched them dragging J.W. from the building. Banyan overheard one of the students say, "Wow. It's too early for an OD, isn't it?"

By the time they got J.W. into the seat, the ambulance arrived. The doctor waved to the two men and said to Banyan, "Go ride with them if you want to come to the hospital. I'm not going to unload him here and put him in the ambulance. Tell them to follow me."

One of the attendants let Banyan into the back of the ambulance, where he sat on a jump seat beside an empty stretcher. They followed the doctor's car, and then at the hospital emergency entrance they unloaded J.W. onto the stretcher and carried him in the emergency entrance.

Banyan followed along, hating the smell of the place, feeling queasy and suddenly relieved that J.W. was out of his hands. He sat outside the room. He was exhausted. When a nurse came and said, "Could you help us get our records started on him?" Banyan followed her numbly to the front reception desk.

"The young man's name?"

"J. W. Hopkins."

"He's a student?"

"Yes."

"Next of kin?" She was small and dark but she had managed to lose almost all trace of Spanish in her accent.

"I don't. . . . Oh, yes, I do know. His father is a minister in Lady, a town out in West Texas. J.W. is one of my students. . . . I just found him . . . injured . . . in my office."

"Do you know where he lives here in Austin?"

"No . . . I never heard him say. The registration office will have all that, I guess."

"All right. . . . Now, what happened?"

Banyan saw again the oddly crumpled figure on the floor in front of his piano. "He was unconscious . . ."

"He fell? Shall I put accident? He must have cut himself somehow," the nurse said. "You have blood on you."

Banyan looked down. It was on his tie and shirt, surprisingly dark. It had dried. Banyan said, "It looks like oil almost, doesn't it?"

The nurse said, "Soak it in cold water. . . ."

Banyan said, "Someone ought to notify his father, shouldn't they? I guess I should do it. My mother knows the Hopkinses. Mr. Hopkins is her minister. I'll have to call him. . . ."

It wasn't possible, of course, to suppress the news of J.W.'s bizarre act, although the dean suggested it. Harriet had immediately told every student she ran into what she had seen in Banyan's office. J.W. had a reputation around the music department as the oddest of the school's oddballs. The first week after he arrived he had stood out on the front steps and played Telemann's Sonata in F minor on a huge harmonica. The fact that J.W. was six foot five, weighed barely 125 pounds, had acne and lank red hair below his shoulders also made him stand out.

J.W.'s act would be remembered the way that the students who jumped from the campus tower were remembered, not by name nor by the reason that drove them to commit their desperate acts, but as legends to dramatize the possible consequence of too much stress, a warning to be repeated in dorms and campus apartments before examinations. If a student failed calculus, there was always the tower. It was a tiresome joke.

Back in his office, Banyan called his friend, Dale Hales, the university psychiatrist. His secretary said he was with a patient, and Banyan asked that the doctor please call him back during the ten minutes before the hour when both of them were free.

Banyan always felt comfortable when he and his wife were at the Haleses' house. Hales mixed the martinis in a large medical

129

flask with tedious precision, and they were wonderfully lethal. "Beats ether, don't it?" he would say when a guest praised his cocktail. Conversation there often was organized around a book that Marsha Hales suggested everyone ought to read. Everyone always did as Marsha suggested.

Still, Banyan delayed calling J.W.'s parents. Now there was a student in his office for her lesson. Tina Wolfe kept squirming on the old chair that Alex had brought up from the basement.

Finally Banyan said, "The bench is gone, Tina. I had it removed. It will not appear in this office ever again."

Tina's eyes filled with tears. "Why would J.W. do a thing like that, Mr. Bonner?"

"Let's concentrate on the Brahms, Tina. Try to get through it now without pausing before the shift. Right there on page three. Here, start at the top of the page. . . ."

As Tina was finishing up her lesson, the phone rang, and Banyan waved her out. It was Hales. He said, "I heard from one of the doctors at the hospital that a music student spilled a little blood this morning, Banyan. Is that what you're calling about?"

"That's it, Dale. He's going to be okay, Dr. Urich says, but did you hear what he did?"

"Nailed himself to your piano?"

"To the bench. One hand. Not to the piano. I found him unconscious when I came in. Look, will you go by the hospital and see him? I've got to call his father and mother, and I want to tell them that the university psychiatrist will be seeing him. His name is J. W. Hopkins. His father is my mother's minister in Lady. I guess I feel responsible for some of this. I helped get J.W. into the music school, and he just hasn't been able to handle the load here. He's got to be eased out, to try some other direction."

"Oh, he's a minister's son. I wish I knew how many problems in the world today are set into motion by ministers. I'll check with the hospital and ask them to let me know when he's able to see someone. They probably want to keep him quiet for a while."

"Thanks, Dale. I'll talk to you later."

"Right."

Banyan couldn't put off the call any longer. Then, he didn't want to go to lunch in the faculty club. They were as bad as the students. They all would want to hear about the piano student who drove a nail through his hand.

Banyan called the dean's secretary and got her to look up J.W.'s home telephone number. He took down two numbers from her and called the church office first. There was no answer. He dialed the second. Mrs. Hopkins answered.

"This is Banyan Bonner in Austin, Mrs. Hopkins. . . ."

"Why, Banyan! Your mother and I were talking about you just the other day, in the Piggly Wiggly."

"I'm calling about J.W., Mrs. Hopkins."

"Has something happened to him?"

"He's in the hospital, but he's going to be all right, the doctors are sure of it. He's had . . . he had a sort of accident."

"He didn't borrow somebody's car? Why didn't he call? Are you saying we ought to come to Austin?"

"I think it might be a good idea. He's lost some blood, but the doctors at University Hospital say it wasn't enough to be really serious, the blood loss. I don't think they even had to give him a transfusion."

"I don't understand, Banyan. Did he fall?"

"He . . . J.W. hurt himself. He drove a nail through one of his hands. . . ."

There was a moment of silence. Then Mrs. Hopkins began to whimper and suddenly burst out, "His father's going to consider that what he's done is a blasphemy unto the Lord Jesus Christ. It'll take us three hours to get to Austin. We'll be right along."

Banyan's hands were shaking as he hung up. There was a knock on his door. "Come in!" he yelled.

He had lost track of time completely. On Friday mornings he had another student at noon. He was a voice major named George Ray Hamilton. The piano lessons were a music department requirement that George greatly resented. He was a tenor. Dottie always insisted that tenors' brains were softened at an early age by the vibrations in their brains that resulted from their own singing. But Dottie was prejudiced. She had once been in love with a famous tenor back in her student days. She was still

131

bitter that he had loved himself so much more than he had loved her.

Like many Texas girls, Banyan's wife had been named after her father. He then spent the next sixteen years of her life telling her how beautiful she was.

The result was that, although Sammie's nose was oddly arched and her chin was weak, Sammie believed that she was beautiful. Her conviction was so absolute that everyone who knew her believed she was beautiful, too. There were no photographs of Sammie. She "didn't photograph well."

Sammie was in her studio, the former garage attached to the house, when Banyan got home after one. She was concentrating on a canvas that covered almost half the floor.

Banyan hung his jacket over the back of a kitchen chair, got out a loaf of bread and put a couple of slices into the toaster. The refrigerator was almost bare. He called out, "Have you been shopping this week? I'm going to have to fry an egg for a sandwich."

"Ugh! You know I hate the smell of eggs cooking!" She was scattering weeds on the canvas. "I want to hear about the student in your office this morning."

"Emily called you?"

Sammie didn't look up. "Nailed himself to your piano? I said I didn't believe such a thing was possible. I said you had a couple of students you wish would get nailed, maybe, but—"

"That's not funny, Sammie. It's J.W. J.W. Hopkins from Lady. Mother's preacher's son."

"Oh, Jesus, a preacher's son. I might have guessed. But I want to hear about the mechanics of it." She was wearing one of his old shirts only half buttoned. She had no bra on and her breasts swung out as she leaned down to shift a small rake that was lying on the canvas. "How does someone nail himself to a piano?"

"It was the bench. J.W. drove a nail through the palm of his left hand and into the piano bench. Then he passed out. I found him there when I went in after practicing up on the third floor. He got into my office sometime last night or early this morning.

. . . I called his mother and they're on the way. I called Dale, too, and asked him to stop by the hospital and talk to J.W. I suspect J.W. isn't going to want to face his father and Dale might be able to help out there."

"Are you through with your toothbrush? The one with the blue handle?"

"Through with it? I just bought it last week. No. It's not even broken in properly."

"Damn. I'm sorry, honey. I needed it so I took it. I'll get you a new one."

"Why in the hell don't you just buy a couple of dozen toothbrushes and have them around when you need a new one? You make enough money. They're probably tax deductible, aren't they?"

"New ones don't work as well. They don't hold the paint the same way a nice old toothbrush does. The old ones begin to spread out their bristles."

"Why don't you buy a dozen or so and boil them in hot water? That probably would make the bristles soften."

Sammie paused and looked up at him. "Good idea! That's a really great idea. You've got blood on your shirt. You are a genius, Banyan! I couldn't possibly do all this without you. . . ." She gestured around at the incredible mess in her studio, a chaos that always made him faintly queasy.

"Meanwhile, I have no toothbrush."

She began to pry open a gallon can of Sears Latex, not listening to him anymore. It was a color that Banyan's father had called "turdmuckledee dun," a mustard. Banyan's mother would squeal, "Oh, Thomas, don't say that in front of the children!" Railroad stations in Texas were all painted that color.

Banyan brought Sammie two pieces of toast on a paper napkin. She wolfed them down hungrily while studying and shifting with her toe the plastic doll arm she had arranged on the canvas. He brought her a glass of milk. She drank it. He said, "Don't forget that Mother and Flannel are coming in this afternoon. Call me when they get here, and I'll come home if there aren't any more lessons."

"Oh, I forgot to tell you. Ellie called. They can't get here in time for your recital tonight, she said. They have some dinner party—you know, yakety, yakety. Ellie running off at the mouth. Ellie insisted that they would stay in a hotel. Does she think that's going to hurt my feelings?"

Banyan put more bread into the toaster, fried an egg in butter and made himself a sandwich. On the dining table was an apple that had begun to shrivel. He ate that. And then he ate four spoonfuls of wheat germ from a jar.

He went into the bedroom and threw his bloodstained tie into the wastebasket. He put his shirt in the bathroom sink and ran cold water over it. He put on a blue shirt. His mother always said he looked wonderful if he had on a blue shirt.

On the way out he looked into the studio again. Sammie was completely absorbed in her painting. She had poured out four different colors into jar lids and she knelt on the canvas, dipping his toothbrush into the paint and rubbing it through a small square of wire screening. He said, "I want to stop by the hospital and see J.W., see if he's conscious."

Sammie said absently, "Give him my love, will you? Oh, and tell him he's not to do that again."

J.W. looked pitiful, awful. He was propped up in the spotless hospital bed, his long hair dirty and lank around his pale, pitted face. He looked old. He opened his eyes. They were dark and sunken, shadows that conveyed nothing, not even pain.

Banyan said, "I called your parents. They'll be here in a couple of hours or so, I'd guess."

"Shit. . . ." He turned his face away in an attempt to hide tears that appeared instantly. "Why the hell did you do that? I've got enough trouble without them. Daddy will come in the door there praying. . . ."

"If praying makes him feel better, why not, J.W.?"

"It adds to my depression."

"You are not depressed. The doctor tells me you're on medication. You're high and happy."

"My hand hurts," he whined. "It's sort of far away, but I can feel it. . . . It throbs. . . ."

"I asked a friend of mine, a doctor, to stop by to see you."

"Your pink shrink? He's already been in. I told him I had been jacking off with my left hand and couldn't stop it so I decided to take drastic measures before all my brains shot out the end of my dick."

"Shut up, J.W. Where did you ever hear anything like that?" Banyan was shocked, but he wanted to grin at the same time.

"You think anybody's going to believe the truth?"

"I might."

"Yeah. . . . You're the one that's always yelling that my left hand is running away with everything. It's always going too fast, spoiling the rhythm, right? Well, it won't anymore. . . . You know?"

"Are you going to blame me for what you did, J.W.?"

"I sure as shit ain't going to take the rap alone for such a really weird stunt. They'll lock me up over in the state loony bin and throw away the key."

"Is it pills?"

"I was down, man. The Bach wouldn't sing. You kept saying it over and over."

"You promised you were off pills. You wouldn't do this to yourself if you weren't popping pills. I hope you're going to see Dr. Hales."

"Can he make me play like Glenn Gould?"

"I'll talk to your father and mother if you want. My mother's going to blame me for this, so between the two of you, you'll be in the clear."

"Tough titty, maestro." He turned his face away again and Banyan left.

Banyan called Dale from his office. "Thanks for going by to see J.W. I hope you'll look after him."

"He's into uppers in the worst way, Banyan. I don't think he's been eating or sleeping for two weeks. He won't tell me what he flies on, but the Demerol isn't helping. That damn fool intern . . ."

"I think after his parents see him he'll be ready for you. They're on their way from Lady. Shall I level with them?"

"You mean tell them he's into drugs? You damn right."

"I mean tell them the kid's not going to make it here. He hasn't got the stuff. I guess I suspected it almost from the beginning. We leaned over backward—I pushed for him. He had a certain moodiness that came through when he played some things. . . . But he's never going to make it as a performer, and that's all he's aiming for."

"Don't you think maybe he already knows it? That might explain the nail through the hand."

"I told you his father was a Methodist preacher?"

"Yes, and I got his records from admissions. It's sad, Banyan. I'll talk to the parents, too, if you want me to."

"Thanks, Dale."

There was another lesson. Friday was his busiest day. A girl named Nannie Knowlton arrived at exactly her appointed hour. She, too, was a voice major, a contralto. She always hit the piano keys with violence. Her eyes were lavender and her breasts large. She inhaled a lot while sitting at the piano. Banyan once saw her unbutton the top of her blouse at the beginning of a lesson when she thought he wasn't looking. Or perhaps she knew he would see her gesture.

The recital tonight was at eight. When would he have a chance for a final run-through? The bottom of his stomach was already beginning to tighten up. Maybe it was the fried egg.

Banyan sometimes felt as if the air in the music building were alive with little black notes that floated like dust in the sunlight. They increased each day until by 11:00 A.M. every practice room and office and studio in the building was fogged with notes. They oozed out from under doors and leaked under windows. By 3:00 P.M. they would begin to fade away.

Next door Dottie's last student had gone. Dottie had put on a recording, as she often did, of Maggie Teyte. "Teyte gets my musical mechanism back on the track after a whole day full of student noises," she once explained.

Why on earth, Banyan wondered, had he said that he would play Chopin tonight? Others on the faculty were noted for their Chopin interpretations and, worse still, Banyan had quickly named one of the nocturnes that he hadn't worked on seriously for years. It was one that too many of the students knew much better than he, one that could easily get him into trouble. He got up from his desk and took the yellow-bound Chopin Nocturnes for the Piano (Joseffy) to the piano. The new chair felt odd. . . . He didn't want to think about J.W. now. The first few measures reminded him of the time that he had first been attracted to this particular nocturne. Like all Chopin, it was for exhibitionists. As a sixteen-year-old he could reach tenths and elevenths and even twelfths with his long fingers, and there were pages of such chords.

His left hand probably would be okay. But the stretches required of the right, especially those that needed a quickness, that must sound absolutely effortless, were difficult, certainly tricky.

He was limping slowly toward the bottom of the first page when the phone rang. "Bonner," he said.

"It's me, honey. Your mother and Flannel are here, and Flannel finally has some gray hair like the rest of us."

"I'll be right home."

"Stop off at Nugent's will you and pick up the chicken? I phoned them to barbecue two for our dinner tonight."

Banyan felt his stomach move uneasily. "Okay. Anything else?"

"No, but hurry up," she whispered. "It's you they want to see, not me." Then in a loud voice, "I'll tell your mother you're on the way."

Banyan hung up and looked at the piano. Should he take the music home and try to run through it there at least once? Sammie hated it when he practiced at home. She would go to the garage immediately. She claimed she could feel his nervousness. That would leave poor Mama and Flannel to hear him flounder through it, and then at tonight's recital they would have to hear a repeat.

He was superstitious. He was afraid not to take the music along with him. He held it to his chest as if it might soak through his shirt and improve his chances of getting through the recital relatively unscathed.

Flannel did appear grayer and thinner than Banyan remembered. And their mother seemed a little less vivid, somehow, than usual. But then she was tired from the three-hour drive to Austin from

Lady. Banyan hugged and patted her. She seemed to have become smaller.

She said, "I'm so excited that we're going to get to hear you play tonight, Banyan."

Sammie said, "Here, give me the chickens, honey. I've got to get busy in the kitchen." On the way out she called back, "Flannel says my new paintings make him uneasy."

Flannel said, "Give me a break, Sammie. I just walked in from a long drive and here was this monster painting on the wall, and you asked me what I thought. I said something dumb, and I'm sorry."

Sammie laughed at his discomfort and disappeared into the kitchen.

Banyan said, "You look wonderful, Mama."

"I look like a witch, and if I'm going out tonight I'd better go lie down. Sammie said I'm in the front bedroom."

"Come on and let's put your bag in there," Banyan said. "Flannel, is the couch okay tonight? Keel is due in any time, and we were going to put him in the bed in the kid's old room."

"Sure," Flannel said. "I always used to sleep on the floor when Papa's relatives came from Silverway. Remember? If the couch is too short, I'll just slide off on the rug."

Their mother said, "You always said you liked to sleep on the floor, honey. I hope Keel's plane is all right. . . ."

"On weekends I still sometimes take a nap on the living-room floor after lunch," Flannel said.

Banyan followed his mother down the hall. "Is the old hipbone still connected to the leg bone?" he asked. She was leaning heavily on her cane.

"It's just like a bad case of rheumatism. When the weather is cold and damp I can feel the steel and nylon socket in there, and I don't like to move it much."

"My mother, the bionic woman."

She giggled. "Papa always used to say I'd have made a right strong old woman if I hadn't had that fall."

Banyan put her overnight bag on the bench to the dressing table.

His mother lay down on the bed with a sigh. "Just put a quilt or something over my feet, will you, Keel?"

"It's Banyan."

"Oh, I'm sorry! I do that all the time. But I know who you are, honey. I've been calling Flannel Banyan ever since he got home this time. I'm going to be jealous lying here because you and Flannel will be talking, and I won't know what you're saying. . . ."

Banyan said, "We won't say anything of importance. You get some rest, and I'll get you up when supper is on the table."

"I won't eat much. . . ."

Banyan closed the door and smiled. His mother always ate twice as much as any one of her sons, except for Field, perhaps. But she insisted that she ate like a bird.

In the living room, Banyan said, "I guess you could have a drink now, if you want."

"Mama might smell it and get upset. She would decide that I was an alcoholic, and I would get lectures on the evils of drink the rest of the week. I don't really need one anyway."

"How does Mama seem to you?"

"She's slowed down since I was last here, but not as much as I expected. Her letters this last year have been full of feeling poorly, but when I got here I guess it excited her, and she's been on the go ever since. On the way here she gave me her old I-don't-understand-what-Papa-and-I-did-wrong-so-that-none-of-you-boys-care-about-the-church inquisition. She did manage to hold off almost a whole day before she sprung it on me this time. Does she still yell at you about the church?"

"I got turned off by all those years I spent playing the organ and listening to the infighting of the preachers and choir directors and Sunday-school teachers. The whole place is a snake pit as far as I'm concerned. It always brings out the worst in people. Mama and I used to get into pretty hot arguments about the church, but she's given up on me. Oh, I've got to remember to tell her about J.W. Her minister's son is in the music department here, and he nailed himself to my piano bench this morning." Banyan pointed to his palm with a finger to show where the nail had been driven in. "His parents probably passed you on the highway."

"Jesus! What caused him to do a thing like that? A nail through his hand?"

"J.W. says it was my nagging him because his left hand had a tendency to run away. . . ."

"You mean he's blaming you?"

"It's okay. I'm sure he laid all the blame on his parents when they showed up at the hospital this afternoon. J.W. is into suffering and he wants to spread the misery around as much as possible. He's popped pills so long he thinks that climbing up out of big black holes is the way everybody spends his time."

Sammie stuck her head in. "Tell Flannel about the gallery."

Flannel asked, "You're going to switch galleries? I thought Harry did very well by you, Sammie. Your show announcements always look great. He spends a lot of money for those color reproductions, and you've always given him credit for making you hot with the Junior League ladies."

Sammie said, "Harry's okay, but I've been there almost ten years, and now he's taking on some newer, livelier kids. The place is getting to look a bit far out for my stuff. The new kids make me look old-fashioned. Anyway, tell him, honey."

"I'm going to retire after next year," Banyan said. "And Sammie wants us to open our own gallery. We're going to call it Uncle Mac's Wagonyard."

Flannel laughed. "You're going to sell carved wooden animals like Uncle Mac used to make?"

Banyan grinned. "Uh-uh. We'll start with Sammie's paintings and a couple of the other painters from Harry's old group. And then we'll go into prints mostly."

"But what about your music?"

Sammie was in the room listening. She stood with a white platter in her hands. Before Banyan could answer she said, "Oh, I guess he'll do what he's always done—pick up a church job and maybe a few private pupils. We won't have to do *anything* if we don't want to. He won't have to take the students that the dean doesn't want, and he won't have to be confronted every year with the new faculty hot shot—who wouldn't even be taking a job in Texas if he weren't third-rate."

Flannel looked at Banyan. But Banyan just sat, smiling. Flannel asked him, "Who's this year's hot shot?"

Banyan said, "You're going to hear him tonight. He's the star of this faculty recital. I'm just the warm-up act and accompanist. But don't you think Uncle Mac's Wagonyard is a great name for a gallery?"

Flannel had a vision of fierce old Uncle Mac, of his gray, unpainted house, of rainwater in an open cistern beside the front porch with its dark smell. Flannel said, "Mama has a postcard from Mittie. She just heard from her. It's in an old lady's handwriting, full of mistakes. Remember her reciting those long, sad poems to us?"

Sammie asked, "Who's Mittie? You and Banyan have too damn many relatives. I've never begun to sort them out."

Banyan said, "Mittie is Uncle Mac's daughter-in-law. Uncle Mac and Aunt Mary took her in after their oldest son Clyde went off with another woman."

Flannel said, "Clyde had a drinking problem. Mittie had a little girl, too—May Annie. I saw her once in Lady after we both were grown. She came by the ranch to see Papa. Did you ever see May Annie as a grown-up, Banyan? I think she lives in Temple now."

Banyan shook his head. "I barely remember her as a little girl."

Flannel said, "She was just a few months older than I am, but when we were little I thought she had all the wisdom of the world. We lived in the country; she lived in town. She knew about what men and women did in bed. Anyway, when I saw her as a grown-up, I couldn't believe it was the same person. . . . No, she was the same, but we had changed—I had changed. She was . . . I realize now that Uncle Mac was some kind of throwback, wasn't he? And May Annie looked like one of those WPA photographs of the dust bowl women. Skinny and gaunt and aging fast. But it was her voice that was the shocker—an old woman's voice, countrified. She . . . she asked me about my church, and when I laughed it seemed to upset her. She never smiled once. Hard as I looked, I couldn't find that bright little girl there at all. You remember, May Annie once wanted to be a movie star like Shirley Temple? Now she's slow and what's left seems sad and life-less, no fun left at all. The juice is gone."

Banyan said, "You don't really remember Uncle Mac, do you? He was exactly that, but with a streak of real craziness, too. The difference was that they were fundamentalists—not in religion, but in their outlook on life. Life was hard, and there wasn't any time or energy for frills like music and reading and art."

Flannel said, "But why aren't we like that, too?"

Their mother was standing in the doorway. "I just knew that you were talking about family, and I can't stand to miss a thing that's being said."

Banyan jumped up and helped her to a chair. "I should have closed more doors."

"No, I couldn't hear anything, but I knew you two were going at it. I think I fell asleep for a few minutes. I feel rested."

Flannel said, "We were talking about Uncle Mac."

Their mother said, "God bless him. A sweeter old man never lived."

"Banyan was saying that they were fundamentalists."

"Why, why on earth did you ever think a thing like that?" their mother asked. "Aunt Mary was a reader in the Christian Science Church, and Uncle Mac's family had been Catholic. He not only gave that up, but he was against all religions."

Banyan said, "I didn't mean a religious fundamentalist, Mama. I was talking about the way they lived their lives. . . ."

Sammie came in to listen for a minute, and Flannel got up to help her set the table.

Their mother's voice took over in the living room. She began to preach. Banyan was sly. He quickly turned her sermon on the vital importance of the Methodist Church into something so extreme that within a few minutes she was laughing at herself.

"Do you mind getting there early?" Banyan asked, as they left the house. He clutched his yellow Chopin to his chest. "Flannel certainly can find the music building. We don't all have to go together in the same car."

Their mother said, "I wish Sammie would come! I can't believe she never goes to hear you play. I wouldn't miss it for the world. I'm so glad that Flannel could bring me."

Banyan asked, "Do you mind waiting around in the hall?"

Flannel said, "We're all ready. Let's all go in Mama's car."

Their mother said, "It takes me so long to walk, Banyan. This way I can take my time, and since we're early we can get seats right up in front in the hall. I know you're nervous, but you won't have to bother at all about us. Flannel will look after me. I wish Keel's plane had gotten here in time!"

Flannel handed Banyan the car keys and then helped his mother into the front seat. She was carrying her cane with the gold top that Horner had given her one Christmas after her accident.

During their last run-through the day before, the Frenchman kept saying, "Don't wait for me," over and over. "I weel move both wiz and against what you and zee piano are doing. Do you understand what I need? I must have zee solid form from you to work against or I cannot build zee castle. . . ." Banyan knew the Frenchman was serious. He must not let him see his smile.

There was an informality about faculty recitals that should have taken the edge off Banyan's nervousness. But tonight the barbecued chicken lay heavily in his stomach. He had eaten so little that his mother had scolded him, but now he was sorry he had eaten anything at all.

He walked down the hall to the arcade that ran along the east side of the music building. It led to the stage entrance of the recital hall. The Frenchman was there, and he greeted Banyan with nods of approval. Banyan was so distracted by the rising nausea that he just smiled tightly. He knew now that he should not be playing the Chopin. He was going to have to take his music out onstage and put it up before him at the piano. The yellow cover was like a flag. His own students would fault him for that. He made them memorize everything that they played in public. Suddenly his hands began to go wet on him. Ugh . . . This was going to be a bad one.

As he got up to go to the door that led onto the stage, Banyan said, "Excuse me," to the Frenchman. "I'll be right back."

The Frenchman chuckled. "It's zee same before zee bicycle races. Zee riders must empty zee bladder."

Banyan realized that he couldn't make it all the way back to the men's room. He let himself out the arcade door and quickly threw up on the gardenia shrub that was there. A repeat performance, over thirty years later, he thought numbly, waiting for another wave to bring up the last of his supper.

He cleaned his face with his handkerchief and then dropped it into the shrubs beside the building. The handkerchief smelled too awful to put back in his pocket. He would have to wipe his wet hands on his pants.

He opened the door and the Frenchman was looking at his watch. "Eet is time for you, Banyan," he scolded. "I 'ope zat you are going to put zem in zee proper mood so zey will be ready for zee castles." He waved his arms in the air.

Banyan managed a weak smile and looked at his own watch. It was five minutes after eight. He should be out there. Cold sweat popped out on his forehead. He blotted at it with the sleeve of his jacket. "Right," he said. The sound came out in an ugly croak.

Banyan pushed open the door and stepped out onto the stage into the blinding lights.

Could they see that he was shaking? There was a splattering of applause—his students, Mrs. Leary from the third floor. He looked vaguely in the direction of the audience and suddenly spotted Flannel, a head taller than everyone else, and his mother. They were right in front. Thank God Sammie never came to hear him play. She would not be a witness to his utter disgrace this time. Only tenure would save him from dismissal after this performance. The hall was packed! Of course, they were all here to hear the famous Frenchman. There were people standing in the back of the hall.

Banyan stumbled as he got to the piano. He put out his music with the pages opened to the proper place, held there by clothespins. Seeing the familiar pins doing their job calmed him for a moment. He sat and ran his hands to the sides of the bench and fiddled with the knobs, lowering the seat just a fraction and then moving it right back up to where it had been. The pedals felt stiff tonight. He pressed down with his right foot to get himself in place and heard a faint sigh from inside the enormous black beast.

It's okay, he said to himself. Nobody is here to hear me anyway, except maybe Mama and Flannel, and they don't care if I miss a few notes. . . . He began to get the light-headed sensation that follows vomiting. He lowered his fingers to the keys and bowed his head.

The rustling in the hall died out. Banyan could hear the waiting. He looked up at the music, "à Mademoiselle Laura Duperre . . ." Why couldn't he focus on the lines and the dots and the row of resting rams along the bottom. Why wasn't he playing Bach? The first note of a familiar Bach prelude always ordained everything else that followed. Bach carried him along.

But this was Chopin, ridiculous Chopin, who did the most outrageous suffering in public, in his music.

Begin.

Was that right? Listen . . . The sounds surprised him. His ears seemed painfully acute. It was too soft, wasn't it? He'd never played lento quite this way before. Was he weak from throwing up? Now it began to sound a little better, didn't it? His tentative beginning had taken the audience by surprise, too. They had to strain to hear him. But they were hooked now, listening. . . .

The music began to take over. He eased his way on into it now, deeper, repeating the phrases as they returned. . . . He began to build, slowly. . . .

When he was sixteen, before his last year of high school, Banyan had gone to Alpine to study for six weeks during the summer with a noted concert pianist. It was Banyan's first time away from home, except for one awful experience at a Boy Scout camp when he was twelve.

Alpine is in far West Texas, with mountains rising above the desert. One of the older students, Dave, took Banyan under his wing. Dave had an old Ford, and on the long hot afternoons, four or five of the students would pile into his car and drive into the mountains where there was a pool, high up in the rocks. It was spring-fed, cool and clear.

After the intense music sessions of the morning, the boys were wild with energy.

Banyan didn't get a haircut nor did he shave the whole summer. There was just the beginning of a soft red beard on his cheeks and chin. The water was delicious. A splash would send a shower of glistening notes into the air. Banyan hit the water with his hands and a whole fountain shot up. "Look," he yelled, "it's the Chopin!" The others caught what he was saying instantly and hooted with pleasure.

Once, one of the boys had brought a camera along. After the swim they were horsing around, posing for pictures. Banyan took two long dry sticks from a yucca plant and made a kind of staff cross that was as tall as he. He stood, put on a sweet smile and said, "Okay, Earl, take my picture."

The result was an Italian sculpture of a saintly looking youth— a John or James or even Jesus, perhaps, with the curling, damp hair and faint beard. Banyan still had the snapshot. To think of it brought back the way the water felt on his skin that day, the sounds of the water and the clear droplets almost in slow motion now in his memory, the sounds of the Chopin . . . He had first played this Chopin that morning when he was sixteen. . . .

There were the chords that required all his fingers but two: eight notes struck at the same instant, clearly. At sixteen he had been thrilled that his fingers could reach them all. The rich sounds he had made seemed small miracles.

Banyan's mother had been genuinely shocked by the snapshot when he showed it to the family. That kind of shock was what he was after now, too. He wanted to be so daring that the whole recital hall of people would be shocked by what he was doing up on the stage. It was as if he were pulling off his clothes now, exposing himself. . . .

He had no real need to look at the music, but he turned the pages automatically. The first part ended and, for some reason, he waited a bit longer to start up the next part. There were three flats now. He would be in three flats until the end. There was not a sound behind him during the pause. Perhaps the hall is empty, he thought, and I'm just imagining this is a recital. . . .

He began the new section with a slower, steadier rhythm. Was it slower than it ought to be? Why was he taking it all so slowly tonight? He was light-headed and possessed by the music, and yet he felt very much in control, too.

With the somber sounds, his mind poked back for darker images, and he saw again the grotesque body on the floor of his office. It seemed as long ago as the sixteen-year-old boy with the watery vision of how a Chopin trill could sound.

J.W.'s hand . . . that was the thing that filled Banyan's vision now, the nail piercing the white palm, turned up, exposing the beautiful script M. And in the center V of that M the rusty nail had gone in and blood had oozed up around it. The fingers had curled inward. It was the pain of it that terrified Banyan. What kind of madness made J.W. inflict this kind of pain on himself? Jesus let them drive nails into His hands, but the pain was so horrible that he had cried out—He believed that God had forsaken Him.

In a distant part of his mind, Banyan was thinking, I'm having some kind of crisis right up here on the stage in the middle of a Chopin nocturne. A fierce Uncle Mac scowled angrily at him. Then the vision of J.W.'s curling fingers with the nail in the palm and the blackening blood flashed in again. It was like being present at the crucifixion. In his mind, Banyan stepped away, and then stepped back again, and the last thing he saw was J.W., twisted, slumped in absolute stillness, all hope and youth gone utterly, J.W. immobilized by his despair, destroyed.

For a moment Banyan thought the hall actually was empty. The last notes had been played. The Chopin was finished. Banyan pulled his foot from the pedal. All vibrations ceased, too. His fingers remained above the keys, not touching, but all sound had now been swallowed up into a kind of eerie silence.

Then someone in the back began to applaud, a kind of tentative splatting sound like big summer raindrops on a tropical leaf. Then another joined in and another and another.

But when he turned he was astonished to see that the audience

147

was standing. His mother, in the front row, looked amazed, and Flannel was grinning up at him like an idiot.

Banyan had never learned how to take a proper bow. He had never really had to, had never given more than a curt nod. Now he saw Harriet on the aisle halfway back in the hall, and he winked at her. He bobbed his head to them all and walked off, feeling their eyes following him. His neck was burning and he knew that his ears were flaming red. He pushed open the door and stepped into the dark.

He was exhausted, totally spent.

The Frenchman jumped up in extreme agitation. He shook his flute at Banyan. "My God," he squealed, "why have you done ziss zing to me? How can I follow that!"

FIVE

Flannel Bonner

FLANNEL, Banyan and their mother came back elated from the recital, teased Sammie about missing the great event, complained because Horner and Field had failed to show up and talked it through again. The brothers finally sent their mother off to bed and then they had a whiskey nightcap.

The alcohol was supposed to help bring sleep, but it just muddled things, Flannel found. Events from both the recent and distant pasts moved in and out of his mind. The couch was too soft. He felt as if he might sink into the cushions and suffocate. A strange pattern of light was coming into the room from above the window blinds, a wall-wide streak with soft, shifting shadows from windblown trees just outside.

But the most disturbing thing was Banyan's heating system. It was a furnace that, at any moment, would kick on with a grill-rattling roar that made Flannel feel as if he were back on the jet that had brought him home to Texas.

Airplanes were time machines, he thought. A dislocation began the moment he walked through the metal-detector frame and down the pale-lit corridor. He became an actor in one of those science-fiction shows on television. Then, as he waited for his X-rayed bag to come along the conveyer, the jitters slipped down and located in his knees, making the joints go soft.

Plane trips set in motion a special kind of nervousness. His jet

151

could crash into another plane as it tried to lift off the runway. That's when most accidents happened. Then what would people say at his funeral?

There were epitaphs on gravestones, but most people were remembered by other things. Flannel thought of the story that had been handed down about his mother's mother's Dutch grandfather, an ancestor remembered only for his gross appetite. Granny used to tell Flannel, "Whenever Grandpa Ogle came for a visit, all the pigs ran squealing under the house." That line was all that remained of Grandpa Ogle, just that single, cryptic family joke.

So Flannel dutifully told his own children, "Yes, we have some Dutch blood. Before the Civil War my grandmother's grandfather, who was named Ogle [that got a giggle] . . . and the pigs ran under the house."

Flannel thought that perhaps his children would tell their children about Grandpa Ogle one day, although he knew that they found the story unremarkable.

Granny's other grandfather was a Scot. "He wore a tartan shawl and a stovepipe hat—in Texas, can you imagine?—and no one ever in his whole life saw him smile."

And Flannel thought, What will be the one line that survives about me?

Banyan's furnace boomed on. All of Flannel's childhood days had begun with the sounds of Banyan at the piano in the distant living room. Flannel believed that, as often as not, Banyan was driven to get out of bed at six every morning to practice just because it made Field furious. Keel could sleep through thunderstorms. And the younger ones, Horner and Flannel, grew up with Banyan's scales and Bach preludes. Flannel was always comforted by the sounds. When Banyan went off to college, mornings were silent and never quite right again.

Field told Mama that Banyan played the piano not to give anyone pleasure, but because he was perverse, because he could dominate the family that way, could hold center stage by playing long and loud.

"What a terrible thing to say about your brother!" Mama said, but she smiled. By that time Banyan was thirteen years old and practicing six hours every day. His teacher told everyone in town that Banyan showed enormous promise.

Suddenly Flannel remembered his companion on the flight from New York, a woman of amazing size, over three hundred pounds, he guessed, with breasts the size of watermelons. He had to stand to let her pass by into the aisle. Her figure, he thought, was like one of those prehistoric clay dolls, a goddess of fertility —all breasts and belly.

In the aisle, she removed her jacket and Flannel saw out of the corner of his eye that she was wearing a bright green T-shirt with a hippo printed on the front. A balloon coming from the hippo's mouth said, DON'T FEED ME.

Flannel remembered some little clay figures he had made one summer day when he was almost six years old. The spillover pipe dripped under the windmill and made a heavy yellow mud, a fine clay. He dug it out with a stick and shaped clay people, one with breasts of perfectly round balls rolled in the palms of his hands and stuck above a bigger ball of a stomach. The father figure was thin and straight with a ball for a head. Flannel lined up the figures on a flat stone and let them bake hard in the sun. Then he borrowed scraps from his mother's quilt box to make little aprons that could be tied on them.

He had a whole clay family finally—a father, a fat mother and several children of various sizes with dogs and cats and chickens. He hauled them all around the house in an old wagon that had belonged to the older boys which he had inherited. One wheelless corner scraped along in the dirt. Flannel took his clay family on a picnic under a mesquite tree and fed them tiny bites of green tomato from his mother's garden.

He took two of the little ones into the kitchen and showed them to his mother who was busy ironing. "Oh, Flannel, how nice!" she said absently. "You really do look after your babies, don't you?"

The next day, Banyan saw him playing with them and said, mysteriously, "The mother looks like she's going to have a baby, Flannel."

But then Keel, who never paid any attention to Flannel, noticed him pulling the crippled wagon with its curious cargo along the driveway. Flannel was on his way to a special place under the porch where he parked his family.

Keel asked, "What is that in the wagon, Flannel?" He was all dressed up in a white shirt and his new shoes.

Flannel said, "It's a papa and a mama and all their little children."

Keel hooted. "Is that what those lumps of dried mud are supposed to be? You made those silly little dolls? Are you playing with dolls? Whooo-eee! I'm going to tell Field and Banyan that you are playing with dolls. Boys don't play with dolls." Keel was fourteen, had his driver's license and was off to pick up a friend and drive around the Lady square. He yelled, "Oh, don't be such a crybaby," as he jumped into the car.

But Flannel did cry, because everything was spoiled. He would never play with his clay people again. He pulled the wagon down to the tank and flung the little figures into the water one at a time, furious with Keel and with himself.

Keel had once had that kind of power over him, Flannel remembered. Keel was the biggest brother. But that incident changed the way he felt about Keel and even the way he felt about his whole family. He began very early to realize that if he ever was to have a place of his own he must get away.

Keel was a spoiler. Flannel thought that probably Keel wasn't always cruel on purpose, but he was insensitive in ways that Flannel had never understood.

When Flannel was about twelve, Keel told him that he was a bastard. He said that Aunt Liz was Flannel's real mother, and that a famous prizefighter was his real father.

Flannel immediately went to find Banyan and ask him. Banyan assured him that it wasn't true because "I remember when you were born, and Mama was big as a house just before you came."

But Keel's story stuck.

One of Flannel's fantasies had been that someday in New York he would run into Geneson in a restaurant. Flannel would walk up and say, "Hey, Mr. Geneson, is it true that you once knew my

Aunt Liz Lacy from Texas, and that you and Riley decided in her apartment that you would lose that first match to him?"

Geneson would turn white, and then Flannel would say, "It's okay, but I've been told that you're my father, so I've always been curious to meet you. . . ."

That's as far as the scene went. Flannel couldn't imagine how Geneson would have reacted to having a middle-aged, bastard son appear out of the blue to upset his tranquil old age. . . .

The heater noise died abruptly, and Flannel started up, wide awake. It's going to crash now, he was certain. When it didn't and he finally realized where he was, he sank back into Banyan's sofa and pulled the quilt up over his head.

At seven thirty the next morning Flannel heard the telephone ring. He had been awake for hours, he thought. A few minutes later he heard Banyan stirring about in the kitchen and got up to join him. Keel had called from the airport. His plane finally had arrived—more than eighteen hours behind schedule.

They drove out to the airport to pick Keel up. In the parking lot and on the way back to Banyan's house, Flannel had a chance to study Keel. He saw a dapper man, straight-backed and trim, who oversaw the arrangement of his expensive luggage in the trunk of Banyan's car.

Keel's blue eyes, reddened only slightly by all the travel and the long delays, had a calm droopiness. His thinning, pale hair was trimmed with naval correctness, his mustache thick but perfectly clipped. At first glance Keel's face had struck Flannel as almost young. Only a close examination revealed the crumbling of its suntanned surface into countless tiny wrinkles.

But all his years hadn't marked him much in the usual ways. Keel was still handsome, and he knew it.

In the early afternoon Horner and Ellie arrived. Flannel followed Banyan to the front door. They shook Horner's hand in turn and kissed Ellie on the cheek. Flannel said, "You look terrific, Ellie." And she did, he thought, much better than she had as a young girl. She was purposely trim now. Her graying hair looked as if it had been expensively streaked.

Their mother came from the living room to the entrance hall, her impatience and excitement obvious. "Is that my baby?" she asked.

Horner grabbed her in a hug. "Well, how's the old fatty grub!"

His mother cried out, "Don't you dare call me that!" But she was laughing.

Flannel was always surprised by the awful things Horner said to their mother—and how much she loved his teasing. If Flannel ever said any of the things to her that Horner did, Flannel was certain she would burst into tears.

Ellie said, "Tell me what you're doing now, Flannel."

"At work or play?"

"Both, I guess."

"At work, it's the same old reports. But at play I've got a comedy with music that I'm trying to get opened. I've been at it for six months, and I may bomb out this time, I'm afraid."

"Broadway?"

"Off-off, Ellie! I'm never going to get anything on Broadway. You're talking about a half a million at least. I can't raise anything like that kind of money."

"I read about lots of off-Broadway plays that are hits and then move onto Broadway. It could happen to you, couldn't it?"

Flannel laughed.

Ellie said, "Why don't you come to Houston and I'll give a party at the club? I'll bet I could raise the money, couldn't I, Horner? You might have to put the play on in Houston first, but they'd be flattered to have a New York producer in town."

Flannel said, "We could call it an off-pre-off-off-Broadway try-out?"

"That sounds wonderful!"

Sammie came from the kitchen. "Is everybody just going to stand here in the front hall? Hi, Ellie."

The sisters-in-law hugged each other. Ellie said, "Oh, Sammie, will you take me to your gallery or someplace? They are just going to sit around and try to see which one can tell the biggest lies about which one's the poorest, and I'm not up to a whole houseful of Bonner boys, pretty as they are."

Sammie said, "Let's wait until Carolyn gets here. She always wants to go shopping when she comes to Austin, and we can go help her spend Field's money."

Flannel turned to follow Horner and his mother into the living room. Ellie asked, "How's Lily?"

"She's great," he said. "She sent her love. . . . She's teaching on Fridays now or I think she might have come this time."

Banyan, Horner and Keel stood with their mother in the middle of the living room as if they had just arrived at a cocktail party. As Flannel came in, Horner said to him, "What kind of a play is it this time, Flannel? Incest and murder again? Can you talk about it in front of Mama?"

"Hey, that's not fair." Flannel noticed that Horner's forehead was lined now. There were squint marks at his eyes, too, sharp ones that looked as if an amateur artist had drawn them on. "This time I'm into sweetness and light," Flannel said. "This young couple has written a sort of play with incidental music that they perform on guitar and harp. It's the book of Genesis with Adam and Eve and Charles Darwin as the serpent. You see? I'm into Biblical stuff, Mama. It's practically an old-fashioned Sunday-school lesson."

"Ah," Keel said. "Nudity will bring them into the theater every time."

"You mean the actors will be naked?" their mother asked.

Flannel said, "Body stockings with fig leafs sewn on top. Actors expect some real money to take off all their clothes. We don't pay enough."

"Well, I should hope so," their mother said. "I've got to sit down."

Banyan said, "Please, Mama, and I'll get some iced tea or coffee or something. What do you want?"

Their mother lowered herself carefully onto the center of the couch and handed Banyan her cane. "Put it somewhere in plain sight so I don't have to go looking all over for it, will you? I always forget where I put it. I wonder where on earth Field is?

I'm mad at him for playing golf yesterday when he could have been here to hear Banyan last night. You really did miss a grand performance, Horner—"

Keel laughed. "It's always the same, isn't it? Mama is always complaining about what we failed to do and worrying about the one who's missing."

Horner asked Keel, "Did you stop by San Antonio and see Gloria?"

"I was running so late that I thought I'd better come on to Banyan's house. I talked to her on the phone. She's fine. She sends her love to everyone."

Flannel didn't believe it. Gloria never thought of anyone but herself. But he was struck by what Keel had said about their mother's worrying. She was the supreme worrier, wasn't she? Why hadn't he realized it years ago? She was the one who had, by example, he guessed, turned him into a worrier, too. He asked, "Did I worry a lot when I was little?"

"Oh, my, yes," his mother said immediately. "I always thought that was why you were so skinny. But your father was thin as a rail until he was past seventy, and that blessed man never worried a day in his life. He knew the Lord would look after him."

"I got it from you, then," Flannel said.

She laughed. "That's right, honey. Blame me for all the bad things. Worrying is a terrible curse. But why couldn't it make me skinny? That's what I'd like to know."

Banyan said, "Maybe that's why you like to live in New York, Flannel. All those neurotic New Yorkers worry so much that you can believe you're almost normal when you're with them."

Horner said, "I inherited more than my share of worrying, too. But I have to keep it pounded down with a lid on it. Lawyers can't show it at the office, and Ellie lectures me if I get too jumpy around her." Flannel thought Horner was beginning to look as if he drank too much. It was his eyes.

The doorbell rang. "Speaking of worriers, and the devil appears," their mother said. Flannel and Banyan laughed at the same moment. Banyan got up to go to the door. "Yeah, Mama," he said, "that Field is a real worrier all right."

Horner said, "Do you suppose that Field has ever worried about anything at all?"

Their mother said, "Why, you boys don't know your brother at all if you think he's like that. Field is one of the sweetest and most sensitive—"

Keel interrupted her with a laugh. "Mama, Mama! I think you're going to overdo it just to make the point that Field is nice about looking after you. . . ."

Carolyn came in first, and Flannel and Horner gave her quick hugs. Keel kissed her on both cheeks. She flushed and turned quickly to her mother-in-law. "Are you feeling okay, Mama-Gran?"

Their mother was distracted by watching Banyan and Field come into the room. Then she said, "Oh, my, yes, honey. Keel's plane was so late he missed Banyan's grand recital, and Horner and Field are such busy men they couldn't get here, but now that everyone's here I guess I . . . Well, I do keep thinking of you boys' blessed Papa. . . . I'm such a lucky, lucky mother, don't you think, Carolyn? Papa was so proud of you boys. But not one of you is the man he was. Did I ever tell you boys that?"

That got a big laugh because comparing her sons—to their disadvantage—to their father was one of their mother's most familiar themes.

The five men, with their mother in the middle of the sofa, settled in. Sammie and Ellie took Carolyn off shopping.

Flannel sat on one side of his mother and Keel on the other. "You two always wanted to get the farthest away," she said to them. "Every family has children like that, I guess. My sister Liz struck out for New York as soon as she had the money."

Banyan sprawled on the rug. Field sat in Banyan's big leather chair with its matching ottoman, and Horner was in a bentwood rocker. He seemed uneasy, as if he thought the chair might spill him.

Flannel said, "I guess I wanted to leave because I couldn't stand all the competition there. I hated going through school in

Lady and always being told that I wasn't as handsome as Keel or as smart as Field or as talented as Banyan. . . ."

There was a long silence and then Horner said that last week he had gone out to the ranch.

"Why, Horner," their mother said indignantly, "why on earth didn't you come see me if you drove through Lady?"

Horner shrugged. "I don't know, Mama. I guess I was looking for something. . . . I spent the night, and then I got cold and drove back to Houston. Your old friendly snake left his calling card again this year. In the closet."

"Oh, no!" She shivered. "It must be some descendant of the original snake by now, don't you think? I always thought of him as the serpent in Papa's Garden of Eden. How long do snakes live?"

No one knew.

The silence that followed grew long. Flannel decided his expectations for this reunion had been too great. They had seen too little of each other during the past decades. There seemed to be no easy way to bridge the vast distances in time, in experiences that had not been shared.

Then gradually conversations began to pick up, but there was more than one, and that annoyed their mother. She had a new hearing aid Field had insisted she buy. She kept fiddling with the little dial on it. Flannel had grown accustomed to talking louder around her, and he did it out of habit. His voice made her jump if the aid were turned up. Banyan and Field spoke so softly that everyone had trouble hearing them. Their mother said that she had to guess what Field was saying most of the time.

Keel asked Field politely about his golf game.

"It's been better," Field said abruptly.

Horner said, "Oh, Field is in hog heaven now that he's playing with the old men. He's become the man to beat in Texas among the over fifty-fives. All my Houston friends come back and tell me what a terror you are, Field. You've made the Bonner name famous on the golf courses at least."

Field grinned and blinked behind his thick glasses.

While the talk about golf was going on, Flannel was telling

Banyan about his daughter Evelyn, who was teaching music to retarded adults in upstate New York. Flannel knew that Banyan didn't approve of using music as therapy, but he was interested in Evelyn, that she was managing to make a living from music.

Keel looked around the room and said, "I wonder if a stranger walking in the door could guess that all of us are brothers? We never did look much like each other when we were growing up, and I guess there's even less of a family look now."

Their mother was annoyed, as if he had somehow begun an attack on her virtue. "Stop that, Keel! I've heard that from the time you boys were just small children, and it's tiresome." Then she began the story of her courtship and wedding, just as if that would somehow clear up the matter of her sons' random appearances.

"I went to Lady to visit my friend Lotte who had moved there when she married. I got there in the middle of June, and we went fishing the next day. Uncle Hank, Aunt Millie, Mr. and Mrs. Leo Slaggs and Wilbur and Lotte. On the way back to town I saw a buggy coming down the street with the most beautiful horse, a red bay, so I said, 'Oh, there's the most beautiful horse I ever saw.' With one voice, six people yelled, 'Thomas!' He turned around, and I met him. He called for a date when we got home and Lotte said he was okay so I gave him one.

"We went to a picture show and the Palace of Sweets. I thought him pretty nice. In the afternoon I had worn a very childish dress, bow tie in back, and all my hair was hanging loose down the back. It was very curly. I was nineteen, and I thought I was grown. He was twenty-five. I didn't stay much longer, but if there was ever a whirlwind courtship that was it. He rode the train to Fort Worth every month and called during the week, brought candy and sent flowers. Remember the red carnations?

"After a few months of that we set January 11, 1914, as the date for the wedding. I was apprehensive, but he had enough confidence for both—and he convinced me. Lindsey Fairman, Hank and Horner McGirk came with him. The rehearsal dinner was courtesy of Aunt Tessie and Uncle Herb who had been married about two years. My very best friend named Mary Pritt was maid of honor. Herb gave me away, and Horner was best man.

"The church was decorated with loads of potted palms and candles. It was held at six, which was dark in January.

"The minister who performed the ceremony was Henry Hogamire, a boyfriend of mine who had only gotten his license the day before—just graduated from TCU. He was killed in a car wreck about two years later.

"I've always regretted I didn't throw my flowers, but your father wanted to take them home to place on his grandmother's grave. She had died about a week before the wedding.

"We were the last couple married in the First Christian Church. It was demolished the next day to build a new one. It was a darling church. The only music was the pipe organ and a marvelous organist. I don't remember what Henry said. He said later he left out 'obey' as he didn't believe in it. Lindsey and Hank were ushers. My suit—no traditional wedding dress—I still think was the most beautiful I ever saw. It was a lovely peacock blue broadcloth with a lace blouse. . . ."

Their mother seemed to run down for a moment. Her eyes were dark with fatigue, sunk deep into her skull. When Flannel was tired, his voice took on a hoarseness that his wife Lily absolutely hated. It made her furious. Flannel's father had the same voice when he got tired.

All of the boys started in talking again, and yet Banyan's living room seemed oddly quiet. Their mother amazed Flannel the way she selected what she wanted to remember for later telling and analysis. Often she picked up only a hint from which she would draw disturbing—but accurate—conclusions.

Banyan, sprawled on the rug, zipped down the top of the weird jump suit he was wearing and scratched the gray hairs on his chest. Field asked, "Do you still have that terrible athlete's foot, Banyan?"

"Yep," Banyan said cheerfully.

"Oh, son, you don't!" their mother cried in horror. "I thought you finally found a doctor who got rid of it."

"He kept my little toes from falling off, but he couldn't cure it."

162

Horner said, "What I want to know is, are any of us ever going to amount to anything?"

Field heh-hehed.

Flannel asked, "Isn't being a big-time Texas lawyer pretty important?"

Banyan said, "Field has managed to get rich right in our own hometown."

Their mother said, "Horner, that's a terrible thing for you to ask! Why, all of you boys are successful. You all have nice families and nice homes. . . ."

Horner said, "And so far none of us has ever gone to jail. Right?"

"Now, you're teasing me," their mother said. "None of you boys is the least bit serious. . . ."

None of them was serious. Flannel was reminded of his daughter Evelyn. They had had lunch a few days earlier and Evelyn was sorting out an immediate problem she was having with a male friend.

"Why is it," she asked, "that when a girl grows up, she looks and acts like a woman? But when men grow up they still look— and act—just like cute little boys?"

Evelyn didn't expect an answer when she delivered pronouncements like that.

"The last time we were all together was in Uncle Mac's wagonyard," Field said.

"Oh, no, honey," their mother said. "We were all together— with Papa, too—right here in Austin during the fifties. I have a photograph of all of us together. Weren't we, Flannel?" She patted him on the knee. Flannel didn't remember.

He kept looking at Keel. Keel seemed to be acting all the time, stiffly, but he may just have seemed that way because of his odd, almost British accent. All trace of Texas country boy had been erased decades ago. "Yes," Keel said to Horner, "I'm going to be a grandfather again. Linda. I may even get used to the idea in a few years."

My God, Flannel thought, he was sixty-three. Why shouldn't he be a grandfather? What a horse's ass. But Flannel smiled at him over their mother's head.

Keel had brought Field some cigars from La Isla, and Field had one of them clenched in his teeth, unlit at the moment out of deference to their mother, who would have said, "Oh, Field, how can such a clean boy put a nasty weed like that in your mouth?" And then she would tell their father's story of why he never smoked.

The afternoon was winding down. Sammie, Ellie and Carolyn were back from the gallery and from shopping, off in the kitchen having drinks, out of sight of their mother-in-law, who pretended she didn't know what they were doing.

Banyan brought in more Cokes and iced tea on a tray that Carolyn fixed in the kitchen. Field said to Keel, "Did you hear that Horner's been made a partner in his firm?"

"No!" Keel said. "Somebody said something about that earlier, I guess, and I didn't get it. Mama must have forgotten to mention it in a letter. That's really fine, Horner. Congratulations, boy."

Flannel had an urge to hit Keel, but it died.

Horner looked down and plucked at a hangnail. "It's nothing. Just twenty-five years of slavery and luck finally rewarded."

Their mother said, "It just happened, Keel. I would have written you all about it. Oh, your papa enjoyed it so much the last time we were all together. He and I talked about it for years."

"Maybe we ought to go to the Driscoll again for dinner tonight, just for old times' sake," Horner said. "I remember now, that's where we had dinner."

"I know that Flannel wants Mexican food," Banyan said. "I already called my friend at Sanchez. The Driscoll's not what it was twenty years ago, Horner. That chef is long gone. But we can go to the University Club if you think Mexican food is going to be too much for this aging crowd."

Their mother said, "Papa always loved Mexican food."

Flannel said, "You don't have to go there just for me. Of course, I never get any decent Mexican food in New York—"

Field said, "Carolyn has her heart set on it, too. She thinks Austin's Mexican restaurants are the best in Texas."

Their mother said, "Oh, good. It's all settled. I didn't want to go to that old hotel dining room." She struggled up from the sofa and Keel and Flannel stood to help her up. "Well, I'm going to see if I can fix this old lady's face as best I can."

Banyan jumped up to help her get started down the hall. He said, "We don't have to leave for thirty minutes or even more, Mama. I made the reservation for seven thirty."

"Oh, my! That's a late supper. Well, maybe I'll lie down for a minute, but don't you boys say anything interesting while I'm out of the room. . . ."

As soon as she was out of earshot, Field said, "I'm going to have a short snort if it's okay with you, Banyan. Can I bring you a drink, Flannel? Keel?"

Horner said, "I'll go with you. Ellie's been too quiet out there."

Keel said, "A finger of gin would be nice. If Banyan has any bitters, just a dash, and no ice."

Field said, "I remember the no ice."

Flannel said, "I'll have lots of ice and a little bourbon and water. Don't you think Mama's going to smell us when she comes back?"

Banyan said, "I'm going to have a beer. Does anyone want a beer?"

When everyone got back into the living room with drink in hand, Horner looked around and held up his glass for a toast. "Well," he said, clearing his throat, "here's to the Bonner boys. I wonder whatever became of them?"

The number one platter seemed to offer a sample of almost every dish on the menu: tamales, enchiladas, refried beans, everything. Flannel ordered it. His mother did, too. "I know I can't eat all of that, but—" She proceeded to eat all of hers, and then she sampled from Keel's plate—he again sat on one side of her—and from Field's plate. He was on her other side. The family had a big round table in a corner of one room, a back room in an old mansion that had been converted into a restaurant.

Flannel sat across the table from his mother, between Ellie and Sammie. Sammie wanted him to go to some gallery in SoHo when he got back to New York and then let her know what it looked like. The gallery owner had written her after a photograph of one of her paintings had appeared in *Oh! Art!* and asked to represent her in New York.

Ellie said, "I don't know how you manage to get so much done, Sammie. Horner's job keeps us going almost every night of the week, and I'm barely able to do all the stuff he expects me to. I'll bet that Lily has a dozen careers, too, doesn't she, Flannel?"

"Mostly she likes to garden," Flannel said. "She claims she's happy as long as she has some dirt to dig in."

Ellie said, "Oh, I remember how impressed the boys were when they visited you, Flannel. They couldn't get over how big and bright all the flowers were in White Plains. They hadn't expected that."

The restaurant was noisy, but Flannel overheard Keel telling a story. "One day when Papa was coming into town, he found a man at the bridge outside Lady, a stranger who was selling hat racks. The man looked destitute, Papa said. His hat racks were made from steer horns—almost longhorns—that had been polished, and they were mounted on a board about eight inches square. The board was covered with blue oilcloth and a little wavy-glassed mirror was tacked onto that. Papa thought it was pretty. It fitted into his notion of what ranch houses should have in them—"

Their mother put her hand to her mouth in dismay. "Oh, son, you mean that old thing!"

Keel laughed. "Well, driving back home, Papa suddenly realized that he was headed for trouble. Mama wasn't going to like it. It had a makeshift look about it. . . . Well, to avoid a confrontation, he just drove straight to the barn and hid the thing under a bunch of feed sacks. A couple of days later when I came home from college for the first time, Papa talked me into giving that hat rack to Mama. She acted thrilled, of course, and we hung it up by the back door in the kitchen—"

"Oh, son, if you only knew how ugly I thought that thing was! I lived with that disgusting piece of trash for years just because I thought you had brought it to me as a present. I almost moved it into town with me, as much as I hated it."

Keel was delighted with the effect of his revelation. His icy-blue eyes were bright, and he made his habitual little nose-shaping gesture.

Field heh-heh-hehed. "Good for Papa. He never got his way about anything, Mama. You wouldn't let him clip the shrubs the way he wanted. You never would let him paint the trim on the house a bright color—"

"Son, your father would have painted our house yellow with blue polka dots, God bless that sweet man. I just can't believe that he would deceive me, Keel. Those cow horns probably came from the Fort Worth stockyards, and I'll bet your father paid that bum plenty for that piece of trash. He could just be a pushover sometimes. . . ."

Flannel looked around the table at the faces. Faces . . . My mama, he said to himself, my brothers and their wives, family. . . . He was reminded of the hallway in his mother's house. She had turned the long, narrow space into a picture gallery. The walls on both sides were hung with framed photographs of family members. There was also a tall, shallow cabinet with blue shelves. His mother had filled the shelves with little metal-framed photographs on legs and easels.

When he was in his mother's house, Flannel would sometimes study the people in this hallway gallery. There was Flannel himself as a baby, framed in gold, solemn, nothing on but a diaper, holding onto the arm of a big chair, barely old enough to sit alone. A larger framed photograph of him as a teenager, all hair and ears, hung on the wall, in a row with his brothers. He was number four in the line up. The photographer had removed his adolescent pimples. Not far away was a photo of Flannel's oldest son Adam, a teenager playing a guitar.

Flannel's father, in a stiff rounded collar, was no more than nine years old in one pre-1900, hand-tinted photo in an ornate frame. He had on a tie and jacket, but he was barefooted. He, too, seemed all ears. Almost all the Bonners had big ears. Nearby was Flannel's other son, Thomas II, older than his own grandfather in this collection of pictures, in a bathrobe, hugging a toy horse and laughing. Flannel's grandfather—his father's father—was a severe-looking young man, and his father's mother, who was unsmiling, were American primitives on their wedding day. Marriage was a grim business.

The brothers were all on display at two or three different ages, too. Horner, at four, sat on a photographer's studio bench with Bisque, the Scotty bitch Aunt Liz brought from New York. Bisque had had puppies and grown snappy. She had to be given away. That was more than forty years ago.

Flannel's brother's wives and children were all in the gallery, too. And even Field's grandchildren, little babies Flannel had never seen because their father, one of Flannel's dozen nephews, lived in California.

All of these relatives at random ages from different times shared this narrow hallway in his mother's house. They looked forward during a common moment, at a photographer as he took their pictures, freezing each one in arbitrary time. This family, this photo gallery family, kept right on growing, adding infants and brides and grooms, in-laws unchecked. The dead lived on there, too.

Flannel's mother had the only record of the family, there in her hallway—chaotic, disorganized, impossible for Flannel to sort out entirely—for anyone to sort out, probably. Flannel had heard that Field's youngest son's wife was going to divorce him. Would her picture be removed? She was a Baptist so no one had liked her much.

In Mama's hallway, time ran in all directions at once, just the way Flannel's memory shifted, constantly. Most of the small, grayed faces triggered different voices, places, events, feelings.

Once years ago Flannel's mother had stopped to admire some pansies in bloom in Mr. Morris's greenhouse out on the Voca road. Flannel was tagging along. His mother said, "See their little faces, Flannel? Pansies always make me sad because they make me think of all the children I wanted to have and couldn't."

Mama said, "Of course I want coffee, but if I drink it I'll be awake all night."

Horner mentioned Uncle Mac's wagonyard. It was the site for every traveling show that came to town.

Keel said, "I thought it was a rotten idea, letting those playacting people put you in a girl's nightgown."

Banyan said, "I remember how beautiful the death scene was with you on that bed in the center of the stage, Horner. I was sure that you would go off to Hollywood and have a career in movies. You'd get rich and then you'd send for me just to look after your cars."

Keel said, "They put lipstick on you, and I was disgusted."

Field said, "I just remember having a laughing fit. Everybody knew it was Horner up there in a nightgown, but Flannel started crying. Aunt Mary Lou was crying. I was really surprised that Papa let Horner be in a play like that."

"I guess I thought Horner really was dying," Flannel said. "I remember they used a lantern slide and had lighted angels on clouds behind the bed, and Uncle Tom knelt down and Horner was carried off to heaven. . . ."

The waiters brought coffee. Flannel let one of them fill his cup. He thought, I'll live it up.

Banyan said, "The road shows at Uncle Mac's were wonderful —or I guess they seemed that way. I remember another time being scared to death by Mr. Hyde with a knife."

Horner said, "I don't remember any of those shows, but there was a later one I remember, and we were all in it. Doesn't anyone else remember Dr. Mental?"

"Mr. Mental—not doctor!" Banyan's face lit up. "Of course! But that was at the high-school gym for Papa's luncheon club. That wasn't at Uncle Mac's."

Horner said, "We all were up there on the stage. Keel was the one I remember best because he marched us up there in front of the audience, and Mr. Mental said that he was going to tell our fortunes."

Keel laughed. "By golly, you're right, Horner. I had forgotten. I can't remember what he said about me, but he said that Field was going to be a cowboy. Would you consider that you are a cowboy, Field?"

169

Field said, "I remember that guy, and he had your number, Keel. He said you had a way with girls, and you turned bright red. That's probably the last time you ever blushed."

Banyan said, "It wouldn't have taken any mental giant to figure that out. You had the look of a skirt chaser early on, Keel."

Field said, "The rest of us looked like kids just in off the ranch, but you were dapper as hell. You must have been about seventeen, and your hair was always slicked down. You had to have a fresh-ironed shirt every time you went into town. It drove Mama crazy."

Their mother patted Keel's arm. "I didn't mind."

Keel brushed the top of his head with an open palm. "I wish I had enough hair to slick down now. What did you do to your hair, Banyan? Do you shave your head?"

"Hell, no. This is what happens when you're a teacher of today's young. It all falls out."

Flannel said, "Mr. Mental was an old drunk. I remember that his breath was foul. But he told Banyan that he would become a pianist, didn't he? That was pretty uncanny."

Their mother said, "You know, Mr. Mental did a pretty good job on all of you boys. I haven't thought of him in years! He said that Flannel would go live far away in a big city, and he said that Horner would be rich and successful."

Flannel said, "Hey, he did better than that with Horner. He said he was going to be a lawyer, didn't he?"

"Wasn't Mr. Mental the one who hypnotized Flannel?" Field asked. "He had that gold watch he swung on a chain, and he tried to hypnotize us all, but Flannel was the only one it worked on."

Flannel said, "Mama will have to sort this out. . . ." Everyone laughed, including their mother. Flannel went on: "You're mixing up two different programs, Field. One of them was a school assembly program, and some hypnotist, an officer from the army base, told me to lie stiff across a couple of chairs, and then he had Banyan stand on my stomach. I couldn't really feel it, but I knew what was going on. I was mad as hell that the rest of you let me be hypnotized. I thought you let me look like a fool."

Horner said, "You never needed us for that, Flannel," and smiled.

Their mother said, "Oh, if only your father could be here!"

"What makes you think he isn't?" Banyan said. "He could be sitting right up there on that sombrero, laughing at all of us and our foolishness." The giant hat on the wall was at least four feet wide.

Horner said, "Sometimes when I'm about to do something I shouldn't be doing I feel like a little boy again, and I hope that Papa doesn't know what I'm up to. I'm sometimes afraid that wherever he is, he knows everything."

"Oh, he does," their mother said firmly.

They ordered desserts. Their mother wanted pecan candy.

After they got back to Banyan's house from the restaurant, their mother hobbled off to bed, exhausted but grinning happily.

The five settled back into their places in the living room. The talk was desultory.

"When I was sick once in the hospital in La Isla," Keel began, "and the nuns there were looking after me, I made a lot of promises that I haven't kept. I guess I thought that something serious was wrong with me. Before that I always felt that it was Papa who had made a lot of promises for me, and that I didn't have to keep his promises. Now, I haven't even kept my own—about not smoking, about other things, trivial things. . . . But I would agree with what we were saying earlier—that I'm not a serious person. I'm too busy making deals. But you're not going to claim that you're serious, Field, just because you put out that newspaper. Your life is mostly those goddamn golf games you play all the time."

Field just smiled, cigar clenched in his teeth. He didn't say anything at all. Flannel thought he saw cords in Field's neck swell.

Horner said quietly, "What I want to know is when will I begin to feel like a grown-up?"

"Boy, I envy you that," Banyan said, "if you really feel that way, Horner. I could use some of the old youthful spark. Every year the students get younger and younger and better and better. Every fall when I hear them audition I feel a hundred years older, with aches in every finger joint. I have to ask myself, What in the hell can I possibly give to kids who already have so much? I feel like a fake most of the time."

Flannel said, "What a bunch of bull! I heard you last night, remember. The mistake you made was in giving up and coming back to Texas. If you had stayed up in New York you could have carved out a career as a concert pianist. Why didn't you?"

"My timing was all wrong. And you're wrong about the career. I never was able to take over a stage and fill it. Keel could do it, if he wanted to, but I couldn't. Can I get another drink for you, Keel? My glass is empty, too."

Keel handed him his glass, and Banyan pushed himself up off the floor.

Ellie wandered in and asked Horner when he would be ready to go to their hotel. He said, "Tell me when you're tired, Ellie. It's only ten thirty. That's barely sunset for you when there's a party going on."

Flannel was sitting behind her, but he thought she made a quick face at Horner. Ellie said that she and Sammie and Carolyn were lying on Banyan's bed watching a television comedy called *The Sound of Canned Laughter*. Banyan came in with Keel's drink and said, "That's Sammie's favorite show. It's about the people out in Hollywood who try out for those jobs as audience laughers on the comedy shows."

Horner said, "You think none of us is serious, Keel, but at least none of us went into television."

"It came along too late," Banyan said.

Keel said, "Do you think Mama was really upset by my hat-rack story? I thought after all these years she would think it was funny. Mama is the only woman I ever deceived, and that's because Papa asked me to tell her I bought that thing."

Field said evenly to Keel, "You learned early to believe them

172

when they insisted that they were wild to get laid by you, didn't you?"

"I've never had a woman who didn't want to be had. I always like to believe that I'm the one who is being used."

Flannel laughed with the realization that he didn't understand Keel at all. Brothers have no inside track on insights.

Banyan rubbed his chest and said, "Keel probably is a poet, don't you think, Flannel?"

Before Flannel could answer, Horner said, "You mean he's really been making poems all these years?"

That got Field's heh-heh-heh started. Field asked, "What's your score now, Keel? Don't tell us you've quit keeping score. By the time you were sixteen you had so many notches in your Boy Scout belt that it wouldn't hold your pants up."

Keel said evenly, "My sex life isn't a suitable subject for an open discussion." But his eyes were bright with pleasure. He assumed that his brothers were jealous. Maybe they were. Flannel guessed that he was jealous of Keel in a way.

But his feelings about Keel stemmed from a memory of the way Keel had looked as a young man, home from college. It was a family joke—the hours Keel spent in the bathroom. Field teased him about it. Banyan complained that no one else could get in. Flannel would wander in and out while Keel was showering, drying and combing his hair, shaving, clipping the hairs in his nostrils and ears, trying to reshape his nose with the odd, pinching gesture that was to become habitual.

Once after Keel stepped out of the shower and dried himself, Flannel watched him take a can of Johnson's Baby Powder and powder himself. Keel rubbed the smoking stuff into his armpits. Then he became so tender and loving in the way he handled his penis and testicles, lifting them gently to pat them with powder, that Flannel laughed out loud. Keel was startled. "What's so funny, Flannel?"

"You really do like yourself, don't you?" Flannel couldn't remember now what Keel said, but Flannel still had that vivid picture of Keel standing there nude before the mirror, totally self-absorbed, patting powder onto himself and smoothing it over his body. Flannel envied Keel that self-absorption, that bliss—maybe even rapture—the pleasure he got from himself.

Jackets were off, belts loosened. Even Keel had unknotted his tie and unbuttoned his shirt collar.

The heavy food, the bourbon Flannel was drinking were taking their toll, cutting him off from the others. He sat, silent. At one point it occurred to him, fleetingly, that if he could just know something about—really understand—one of these four other aging men in this room, then he might have an important clue about himself, about what he should have expected out of life for himself. Maybe all he could get from them was a hint of where he would be three years from now (Banyan), five years from now (Field) and seven years from now (Keel). But Flannel wasn't ever going to be a dissatisfied music teacher or a gamesman or a calculating womanizer. And he never had been where Horner was now: a serious drinker with a job that frightened him. That wasn't all that they were, of course. Was it? Flannel was certain that there had to be much more to them, these sprawling, half-dozing brothers. . . .

Banyan and Flannel were talking. There were lots of long pauses. Flannel said that because of Banyan, Flannel had never managed to come up with any original obsessions of his own. All of the ones that he had enjoyed through the years had been handed down, just like Banyan's pants and jackets, when they were growing up. Banyan had introduced Flannel to vague, soothing Debussy and left him there while Banyan then moved right on back to Bach. Banyan once had played a recording for Flannel of Carl Sandburg singing "God damn your eyes" so that Flannel made a great effort to go see the old man on tour, up on a stage with his guitar and powerful, hoarse voice. Sandburg sang and read his poems, and Flannel thought he was a wonderful performer. He may have been a real poet, too, but his simplicity made Flannel uneasy.

Flannel was so absorbed in his daydreaming that he missed whatever it was that Field had said in that soft voice of his, or what it was that Keel may have thought Field had said. They all were tired. But there must have been something that set them off.

There was a rush of movement, the solid whump of a heavy blow, and Field's low voice grunted something that sounded like, "Why, you old fart!"

Banyan leaped up and Flannel followed, struggling to his feet and slopping his drink over his hand and onto the coffee table. Keel and Field squared off, crouched. Keel said, "You always did resent it, didn't you? You never have given up on it!"

Horner, who had been dozing drunkenly in the bentwood rocker, started awake and said, "Keep it down! You guys are going to wake Mama!"

There had been another fight, Flannel suddenly remembered. At the ages of sixteen and thirteen, Keel and Field had had a fight out in the backyard under Mama's clotheslines. Flannel had heard the first noises and rushed out the kitchen door to see them squared off, glaring at each other. Their eyes had a kind of hatred that had frightened Flannel and held him fascinated. They had pushed each other to the ground. Shirts were torn, noses bloodied. Keel, with his experience on the football team, was in better shape, but Field had a kind of cold fury that made him formidable. Field was furious then, and he was furious now.

But back then, Mama had followed Flannel out of the house and yelled for Papa who came running from the barn and separated them.

Field suddenly remembered his glasses. He pulled them off and handed them to Horner. Flannel laughed, but no one else did.

Banyan said, "We'd better get out of Sammie's living room. Let's go out front."

Flannel said, "It's almost midnight, Banyan. Tell them to sit down and cool off."

Keel reached over and slapped Field across the face, turned and strode through the entrance hall out Banyan's front door and into the night. Field yelled and lunged after him, but he couldn't see without his glasses and he stumbled against the coffee table, went down on one knee and came up red and frenzied.

Horner's face took on a look of panic. "What in the hell are you doing? My God! You're sixty years old!"

175

Field said, "I'll bust his fucking head in! I'll stomp him! I'll—"
He was out the front door, too.

Flannel felt a rush of excitement, of pleasure even. He said to Horner, "Hey, this is a fight that started before you were born."

Banyan's eyes were bright, and he was grinning. "Come on," he said to Flannel and Horner at the front door.

There was plenty of light out in front, from the moon and from a streetlight across from Banyan's house. As Flannel came out, Keel was saying, "Papa's not here this time to save your fat ass."

Horner said, "Jesus, Flannel, what in the hell is it all about?"

"It's about being mad at somebody for fifty years down inside your gut . . ." Flannel laughed, but tried to keep it soft. He was ashamed of the joy he felt, at the sheer craziness of what Keel and Field were doing. ". . . and they never really found out which one was top dog."

Horner said, "They aren't fighters! They are old men, for Christ's sake. We've got to stop them. What if one of them gets hurt? Keel looks as if he wants to kill—"

Flannel moved away from Horner. Banyan was out near the street. Keel and Field were circling in the middle of the lawn, facing each other, crouched uncertainly, neither boxers nor wrestlers exactly.

Suddenly Keel reached up and untied his tie and flung it over to Horner. His voice was unnaturally loud. "You never did learn your goddamn lesson, did you, snot-nose?" he said to Field.

Flannel liked that. He hadn't heard anyone call another person "snot nose" in thirty years.

Field said, "Just who in the hell made you the teacher?" He sounded nasty and mean, meaner than Flannel had ever imagined he could be.

Keel threw out a fist wildly and missed. "What a tub of lard!" he yelled.

Field muttered something Flannel didn't catch. Field moved in, grabbing and clutching, ignoring the blows that Keel was throwing at his head and chest. Keel tried to push him off. "Fight, you fucker!" Keel yelled. "What the hell do you think? . . ."

Field was holding on. He wrapped his arms around Keel's

waist, hugging him, bearlike, so close that Keel's blows were ineffective.

Keel kicked and slipped and pulled them both off balance. They fell, slowly at first, then grunting as they hit the ground with a solid thud. Flannel was sure that Field had crushed the breath out of Keel.

But Keel squirmed out from under, flailing away and yelling more curses. "Stand up and fight, you turd! You shithead! This is a fight, goddamn it!"

Field struggled to his feet, too. With his face turned up to the light, Flannel could see that Field's nose had begun to bleed, a black, liquid shadow spilling down across his mouth. He wiped his nose on his sleeve and said, "I beat your ass before, and I'll beat it again. You can go ahead and fuck every piece of pussy in the world for all I care!"

Keel hit at him and clipped an ear. "Oh, ho! You're still crying about that! Oh, you baby. You never have got enough, eh? And it's all my fault! Crybaby!"

Sammie appeared in the doorway in her robe, with Carolyn and Ellie behind her. "What in heaven's name is going on?" Sammie hissed. "Are you playing some kind of game? You're going to wake the neighbors, Banyan. Their lights are coming on now. Stop this!"

Field said, "I'll finish off the old fart right now." Again he moved in to grab Keel.

But Keel slipped away, dancing on his toes. "Fight, Field! Can't you put up your fists and fight! Didn't they teach you anything in that goddamn army?"

Field aimed a fist as if it were a battering ram and lunged at Keel's chest. Keel moved, but not quite quickly enough. The blow struck him on the shoulder, throwing his head jerkily to the side. The shock of it infuriated him, and as soon as he regained his balance he crouched again in his boxer's stance, punching away at Field, who just stumbled backward, away from the blows.

They were incredibly awkward and inept and slow. Horner said, "Why don't you guys stop it now? Enough is enough."

Flannel said, "Let them go." Already, the story of this night

177

was beginning to take shape in his mind. Lily wouldn't believe him when he told it. She thought Keel was a stuffed shirt.

Suddenly Field must have decided he had had enough of the rain of fists. He grabbed at Keel, and again they fell onto the lawn. But this time Keel was on top. He moved quickly astride Field's stomach and began aiming blows with his fists at Field's head.

Field grabbed one of Keel's arms and jerked it, throwing Keel off balance long enough so Field could push him off and struggle to his knees.

They were both on the ground panting now. Field was making a kind of terrible, harsh, bubbling sound. But Flannel thought that Keel had been hurt worse. The arm that Field had twisted seemed to be out of commission.

Keel wouldn't give up. He crawled back, hitting at Field with his good fist.

When their mother's voice rang out, it startled Flannel. He turned to see that she had pushed aside the other women and was out the front door, a tiny pale ghost in a trailing lace peignoir. "Boys!" she cried, in a voice that she once used to sing "Open the Gates of the Temple!" in church. She tottered, caneless, off the front steps onto the lawn. "What on earth are you boys up to? I heard the most terrible language!"

Keel said, "I'm just teaching Field a lesson, Mama. He's been in need of it all his life, the smart ass!" He slapped at Field again.

Mama yelled, "Why are you just standing there, Banyan! Flannel! You get in there and stop your brothers from making fools of themselves like this. Why, I never! Thank God this isn't happening at home. I'd be disgraced forever. Banyan! This is your house. Stop them right now!"

Banyan began to laugh. "I can't, Mama. They're older than I am."

Flannel was laughing, too, but he didn't want his mother to hear him.

"Well," Mama said, "so I have to stop this foolishness myself? Would you boys beat up a crippled old lady who's almost eighty!" She started toward them.

Field mumbled, "You are eighty-six, Mama, and you keep out

of this." He hit Keel on the shoulder to make his point. Keel moaned and struck back instantly, dodging away on his knees as he did it. They looked like ancient, wounded animals.

Mama said, "I just can't tell you how disgusted I am. You wouldn't be fighting this way if your father was here, God bless him. That man never had a fight in his life. I just can't believe that sons of mine—grown men—would resort to fisticuffs to settle some imaginary differences."

Ah, fisticuffs. What a nice word! Flannel loved the way his mother used words from the past.

Keel said, "Field has been jealous of me all my life, and he won't let me alone. He just needles and needles and makes cracks about women, and I'm goddamn sick and tired of it." He hit out in Field's direction. There was a small thud of contact. Both had struggled to their feet again and were stumbling in a circle.

Mama said, "I believe that both of you have been drinking. This is just the kind of behavior that drinking encourages. You boys think I don't know what goes on when I'm not around, but I just pray to the Good Lord that you don't all end up drunks like my blessed father. I always taught you boys to play pretty together. I just can't believe you'd get out here in the middle of the night and fight like thugs!"

Carolyn came out and stood behind her mother-in-law. "Field? You better come in now. You are just a mess."

Keel said, "Yeah, Field! You better go in now."

Field grabbed for Keel again and for a third time they fell, slower than before, flailing at each other, except that one of Keel's arms wasn't working at all. Field was bleeding from the mouth as well as from his nose.

Their mother took a few more tottering steps toward them. "What kind of example is this for you to set for your little brothers, Keel! You get right up! Right this minute!"

A man and a woman in the house across the street came out on their lawn, and then Flannel suddenly saw the flashing red lights on a patrol car as it pulled silently into Banyan's driveway.

"The police!" their mother yelled. "I never thought I'd live to see the day my boys would wind up in jail!" She made a terrible sobbing noise.

Banyan strolled over to the police car. "Good evening, officers," he said politely.

The policeman at the wheel said, "We got a complaint about noise and cussing coming from your house. Some of your neighbors are unhappy about it."

Banyan said, "My brothers are here visiting in Austin for this little family reunion, and they just had a few differences that they thought they needed to get ironed out. . . ."

Their mother called out, "Come get them, officers! Take them off to jail where they can cool off. They need to think about what they have done to send their poor mother to an early grave!"

The officer said to Banyan, "Aren't you the man that plays the organ at my wife's church?"

Banyan said, "Uh-huh, probably. I do that sometimes. University Baptist. I teach music at the university."

The officer said, "My wife just loves the way you play 'Wagon Wheels.'"

"Did I play 'Wagon Wheels' in church?"

"Well, it's probably not the real 'Wagon Wheels,' but it's an Offertory song that sounds just like 'Wagon Wheels,' with a nice beat that I can tap a toe to."

Banyan said, "Well, please tell her I'll play it for sure next Sunday."

Their mother said, "The police are here to take you boys away!"

The officer said, "It looks to me as if your fighters have pretty much pooped, don't you think?"

Banyan laughed softly. "We'll take 'em in and put 'em to bed. This fight started back when they were teenagers, and it's just never going to end."

"Well, if you can get the old lady quiet, we don't need to mess into family business. You don't have any guns around for them to get at?"

"No guns."

"Keep 'em away from the kitchen knives until you're sure they've cooled off."

"Right, officer."

The police car backed out silently, its red lights no longer flashing.

Their mother yelled after them, "Where are you going, officers? You've got to put a stop to this mayhem!"

Flannel said, "I think Keel and Field are just about finished, Mama."

Keel lifted his usable arm and swung it slowly at Field. There was almost no sound when his fist hit. Still, Field let out a terrible rattling groan and reached out, falling to his knees at the same time, bringing both of them to the ground once again. "Your ass!" he said.

"Oh, son! You mustn't talk that way!" their mother said.

Banyan said, "I think it's all over. Flannel, why don't you take Mama back in the house and get her tucked into bed?"

Flannel helped his mother back into her bed in the guest room and then had to fumble through her overnight case looking for the pill she wanted to put her to sleep. For her trip, she had just taken the forty or so pills she thought she needed for the two-day visit and put them in an envelope. There were white ones in three sizes, pink ones, yellow ones, capsules and big shiny brown ones. Flannel lined them up on the dresser top. "Are you sure that your sleeping pill is the smallest white one, Mama?" Flannel wondered what would happen if he gave her a pep pill by mistake. She was talking like a crazy woman right now and sounded as if she could go on until morning.

"I guess I thought that you older boys got all that fighting out of your systems during the war. I just don't understand why boys have to try to settle things by fighting! It doesn't ever really settle anything—not really, does it? The loser just goes off and sulks until he gets a chance to fight all over again. Why, I thought those boys were the best of friends! Field handles all of Keel's banking and business in this country. . . ."

"It's okay, Mama. They are devoted to each other. Is it this white pill with a tiny *T* on it?"

"That sounds like the right one. Will you get me a glass of water, too, honey?"

Flannel went into the kitchen. Sammie was eating a bowl of cereal. She said that Banyan had taken Keel to the emergency room at the hospital. They thought his shoulder had been dislocated. Horner and Ellie had gone off to their hotel. Sammie said that Ellie was considerably shaken by the fight, and Horner had sobered up.

Carolyn had Field in the bathroom, cleaning him up. His upper bridge, Sammie said, an expensive piece of dental work, had been ruined, and he was a bloody mess. "But he is cheerful," Sammie said in wonder. "The old fool thinks he won because he put Keel in the hospital."

Flannel thought of the look on Field's face. Once Flannel had ridden around on the golf cart and watched Field in action. "He likes to win," Flannel said to Sammie.

Flannel took the water back to his mother who was all propped up on pillows, her eyes dark and hidden in the sunken recesses of her skull. She put the pill on her tongue and gagged on it—for Flannel's benefit, he thought.

She said, "Sit here for a minute until I begin to doze off, will you, Banyan?"

"I'm Flannel," he said.

She laughed softly. "Oh, I know who you are, honey. I just mix up the names. You know that."

"It's okay," Flannel said, and he sat at the foot of her bed. Sammie had photographs of her mother and father on the walls of the guest room. Her father had been an oil speculator, wealthy sometimes, wealthy enough to send Sammie to a private boarding school in Dallas and to the Art Institute in Chicago. Then shortly after Sammie married Banyan, her father died. He was a short man and he had smoked cigars. Flannel had met him only once.

Flannel's mother was saying, ". . . I'm glad Papa wasn't here tonight for this mess. I just don't understand it! Not for one minute! Two grown men behaving that way. And brothers! Why, when I saw the two of them out there—the name-calling, the hate and meanness—I thought of Cain and Abel right out of the Bible." Without pausing even for breath, she managed to shift the subject. "When I was a little girl I wanted desperately to be a boy. Did I ever tell you that, honey?"

"Yes, Mama."

"I guess I thought my daddy would love me more if I was a

182

boy. Every time one of those little dusty whirlwinds came down the road, I'd run and try to get into the middle of it so I'd turn into a boy. Isn't that silly? I learned a lot about boys after you children came along, and the more I learned the less I understood. Boys just don't ever grow up, do they?"

Flannel laughed. "Well, some of the parts begin to wear out."

"I did so want your papa to have a daughter. I guess I never said it to any of you. I thought Field would be a little girl, and then we'd have a perfect little family. When Papa and I turned out to have two boys, I thought we'd try one more. It surely would be a little girl. Then after Banyan we never intended to have any more children. And you came along, and I was just determined in my own mind that you'd be a girl. Hah! You fooled me, too. So by the time Horner came, Papa and I just knew all along that he would be another little boy. And, you know, it's lucky, because by that time I had just gotten to where I was crazy about little boy babies!"

Flannel saw a big tear appear on her cheek and roll down. "You want me to turn out the light, Mama?"

"I want you to explain why you boys drink whiskey and ignore the church when you know how Papa and I feel about those things. How could your brothers fight each other—like animals! You know it was the whiskey, wasn't it? Your father was the most gentle man who ever lived. . . ."

"I guess we got our meanness from your side of the family."

His mother snorted a short laugh, waved a slow slap at him and then sobbed a tiny sob with sniffles. "Those old fools! Why, honey, just think of it! They're both over sixty years old, and behaving like young dogs. What on earth were they fighting about, do you know?"

"The same thing they've always been fighting about. Which one is bigger, stronger, smarter, quicker—which one is the better man."

"Well, that's just downright disgusting, isn't it?" She snuggled down into her pillows and pulled the covers up to her chin. "I'll bet it was that Mexican food we all ate for dinner. Poor Field always did have a delicate stomach. I bet that hot pepper seasoning just set him off. . . ." She giggled sleepily.

"Good night, Mama. Sweet dreams. . . ."

"It makes me wonder if you older boys would sell off your little brother into slavery in Egypt. Are my sons capable of that kind of . . . The world just never changes, does it? Boys will be boys. The Bible just says it all. . . ."

Flannel turned out the light on the dresser. Then as he was at the door, his mother said, "Papa was so generous to take Liz's baby and give him his name. Papa and I were just starting out, too. It's that fighter's blood—it was just inherited by Keel, and blood is what tells after all. . . . It didn't make any real difference what Papa and I tried to teach him, did it?"

"Well, Mama always needed to believe that we were better than other people, and somehow she managed to convince me," Flannel complained.

Banyan said, "Papa, thank goodness, never believed her for a minute. He used to say we were just common as hen's teeth. Keel and Field never bought Mama's grand illusion at all. . . ."

Banyan and Flannel sat in the kitchen at his white breakfast table. Banyan was in his shorts. The house was quiet. Sammie and Carolyn had made up a bed for Flannel on the living-room sofa, then gone off to bed. Carolyn reported back once that Field was snoring like a bull, and she wasn't going to get a wink of sleep.

Keel was in the hospital for the night. His shoulder had been pulled into place and taped. The doctor had given him pain-killers to knock him out.

Banyan and Flannel were dampening the last embers of their excitement with the last of the bourbon.

Flannel said, "I was ashamed at how much I enjoyed seeing them go at each other."

Banyan laughed. "I saw you while it was coming on. You didn't notice, did you? They'd been working up to it all day. I never would have thought at this point in their lives it would come to an old-fashioned knockdown—and then drag out the way it did."

He rubbed the gray hairs matted on his chest and grinned. "I thought of Wagner's Ring while it was going on. There was a kind of grandness about it all—two aging males still willing to try to beat the shit out of each other."

"When the police car came up . . ." Flannel began to laugh. "Do you really play 'Wagon Wheels' at church?"

Banyan shook his head. "I don't know what the hell he was talking about. . . ." They talked through the battle again from the beginning, trying to turn it into an epic—or at least into a family legend that would be told again and again. Flannel said, "I'll bet Mama's going to have a wonderful version of this night for Aunt Dori and the others, don't you? She may even wind up some kind of heroine and claim she had to stop it all by herself." Under the talk, Flannel kept wondering if Banyan knew that Keel was the adopted one.

Banyan emptied his glass and got up to take it over to the dishwasher. He had always been as thin as Flannel, but now Flannel noticed the beginning of a paunch. "You're finally getting some weight, aren't you?"

Banyan pooched out his stomach even more, the way he used to do when he was a teenager. He said, "Those old fools . . . They really do love each other, don't they?"

He patted Flannel on the head and went off down the hall, leaving Flannel to finish his drink, turn off the lights and put himself to bed in the living room.

Flannel had just pulled the sheet up over his shoulders when he heard Banyan in the doorway. Banyan said, "Are you all set?"

Flannel took a deep breath. "Did you know that Keel was the one?"

"Keel . . . was the one what?"

"Mama said tonight that Keel was the one that Aunt Liz had."

Banyan was a silent shadow in the dim light that spilled down the hallway behind him. "I guess I never thought about it much."

"I always thought it was me . . . or I did when I was feeling that I didn't fit in."

Banyan snorted softly. "I've told you and you forgot. I saw you lying next to Mama right after you were born. You had little black

185

beady eyes, and I thought you were a 'possum. I wanted Mama to show me your tail."

They hadn't talked like this in the night, confidences in the dark, since they were teenagers, sharing the same room. "I've got big ears, too," Flannel said. "And I guess I should have known all along that it was Keel. It is true about Aunt Liz and Geneson. I've got the old newspaper clippings about the lawsuit she filed against him. It isn't just a story Mama made up." Flannel waited, but Banyan didn't speak. "Now I haven't got an excuse anymore. . . ."

Banyan laughed.

"You don't understand," Flannel said. "It means I have to start all over."

"Start what all over?"

"Trying to find out who I am. . . ."

Instead of answering, Banyan said suddenly, "Did you know that Field's favorite movie star was Kathryn Grayson?"

Flannel's mind went blank, sifted through a lot of information and finally conjured up the tiny brunette with the big eyes and the cute nose and the trembling voice. "Kathryn Grayson?"

"Night," Banyan said and disappeared again.

When their mother was younger, Flannel thought, she probably had looked a lot like Kathryn Grayson. And, of course, both of them were singers. Only Banyan, of all the people in the world, could understand how much pleasure Flannel would get from knowing about Field's great, romantic passion for a movie star. That was an unlikely piece of information from the past that Flannel could grasp, could cope with and even enjoy. For the moment Flannel felt snug, no longer totally alone and isolated.

Someday, if he lived long enough, Flannel hoped that he might come to understand the intensity of feeling that had brought on the fight tonight. Why had he never hated—or loved—like that? And he would even find a way to let himself think about what his mother had said about Keel. Truth, that kind of terrible truth that alters the past in just a few words, was impossible to comprehend right away.

There. That was the best he could do at this time of night. Now he would sleep. . . .

But his mind wouldn't give up. He thought of his father. Just the day before, his mother had insisted that they stop off on the way to Austin to visit his father's grave.

The new cemetery was across the highway from Field's golf course. The first Lady cemetery on the east side of town had filled up years earlier. Flannel as a child had liked visiting that one because some of the graves had stone angels.

This new cemetery seemed desolate. No trees yet. And there were no angels. Was sculpture no longer stylish? Or perhaps it was too expensive now. His father's stone was easy to find—a big rectangular block of polished red granite. Red was Thomas Bonner's favorite color. Cut into the stone under his name was: LET NOT YOUR HEART BE TROUBLED.

Flannel's mother talked all the time. She always had. But it was never altogether purposeless. Indirect sometimes. Tentative. But there were messages flowing, things that she thought were important. Sometimes Flannel knew that what she said was intended not for him at all, but for his wife or for one of his children or even for one of the brothers.

She said, "I always thought that you and Horner came along so late you never knew Papa as well as the older boys did. I know we weren't as much fun. Your father was always cutting up with the other boys."

Flannel braked the car, got out and opened the door for her. She swung her cane out first and slid carefully off the seat. "Your Papa always used to say if I hadn't slipped and broken my hip I'd have been a right spry old lady."

She used her cane as a pointer. "Do you like the new vases?" White marble urns had been added to each end of the red granite slab. When Flannel didn't respond immediately, she knew he didn't like them. Flannel still would be honest sometimes—and even mean—to her. She plunged on. "The trouble is that Eula Lee saw them, and she's ordered two for her mother's stone right over there. And Mrs. Snell said she thought they were so pretty she would get a pair for the stone on her lot. The whole place is going to have them. . . ."

The day was clear and dry. There was a heavy coat of white

dust on the red granite. The Saint Augustine grass on the plot was just beginning its early March green-up.

Flannel's father had died in February 1969 of a stroke—was already dead when Field's wife, Carolyn, telephoned Flannel. He flew out of New York the next morning, rented a car in Dallas and drove home. The car radio seemed to have only one song on every station: "Like a Bridge Over Troubled Waters."

When the coffin was brought from the church, "The heavens just opened up, and it poured rain. Just fell in buckets." His mother always described rain that way. Because a rain like that happens so rarely in West Texas it has an exhilarating effect. Flannel remembered times when he was little that his mother would get so excited during a sudden rain that her face would become terrifying. She would flap her apron, yell happily, run out of the house and get soaked.

At the funeral, brown waters ran into the rectangular grave. It looked too short for his father. Flannel looked up and noticed faces of people around the grave who were all familiar from his childhood, but they were older, smaller somehow, shrunken. . . .

Now the whole dusty plot looked even smaller, not nearly big enough for his very tall father.

"I hope you don't mind stopping off out here, Flannel. I just couldn't stand to think of this grass so overgrown like this, and I can't get down to clip it. Here, if you connect the hose over there, I'll water Papa and old Mrs. Davis next door. Her son is just pitiful these days. Did I tell you? I don't think he draws a sober breath from dawn to dark and then at night he gets down to his serious drinking. . . ."

Flannel connected the hose to a faucet and then got the clippers from the car. They were the same old clippers that his father had used to trim his mother's flower beds. She said, "You know what a trimmer Papa always was. He would have turned every shrub we had in the yard into an animal shape if I'd have let him. That's the way, honey. Just clip those runners off the curbing and away from the stone there. Then I'll wash off the dust and we'll go."

Suddenly she seemed in a hurry to leave.

While trimming the grass from the red granite, Flannel's mem-

188

ory slipped easily into the past. After Banyan went off to music school, Flannel was the oldest son left at home. It fell to him to shave his father's neck every Sunday morning before Sunday school. His father would sit sideways on a kitchen chair and Flannel would make an elaborate business of getting a pan of hot water, a washcloth and his father's old safety razor. The silver plate on his razor was worn off and the brass underneath was bright and smooth. Flannel was about eleven at the time. He especially liked opening the fat jar of Burma-Shave and smearing on two fingers worth of heavy white cream.

The part of his father's neck above the collar was as red and dark as his granite gravestone, but rough and ringed with old-man wrinkles. Below the collar line the skin was absolutely white and smooth. The hairs were white, too. Flannel had to be careful of the deep wrinkles. The shaving took only a few minutes, and then Flannel wiped off the remains of the cream with the hot washcloth. He was always neat. His father would say, "Feels just like being in Panky's chair." Panky was the barber in Lady.

His mother said, "That looks just fine, Flannel. You don't need to fuss with the trimming anymore. Here, turn off the water for me, will you, and then roll up the hose? I used to keep a hose out here so everyone could use it, but somebody took it so now I have to carry one in the car. Can you imagine anyone taking a hose from a cemetery?"

Flannel started to tell his mother about remembering the shaving sessions on Sunday mornings, but she was talking about how Banyan might worry about them if they were late. Flannel wasn't certain that he could tell her without starting to cry, although he wasn't upset by the memory. It had just been vivid, and his father had been alive, warm.

Even with a heavy coating of Burma-Shave, his father's skin had been so rough that the razor had sort of skipped along. Flannel remembered exactly the sensation of the blade scraping across the weather-beaten, granite-red hide.

Flannel carried his mother's bags out to her car and stood there with Field. Field was driving her back to Lady, with Carolyn following in Field's car. His nose was puffed. There was a red bruise under one eye, but he had shaved carefully and that had removed the dark beard shadow that sometimes colored his face. He looked much younger this morning. He insisted he felt great. But his thick, horn-rimmed glasses set him apart as always, Flannel thought, distanced Field from everyone.

Flannel said, "Mama seems okay this morning. When she writes us she always lists her ailments because they are so much on her mind, but she seems just about the same to me."

Field nodded. "She always gets excited when you come down, and she'll be exhausted for a couple of weeks after this, but it'll give her something to think about."

"How's business?"

"Carolyn and I keep busy enough. Lady never is going to be a boomtown so I guess I won't have a lot of the big newspaper chains hanging around, trying to buy me out."

Their mother hobbled out on her cane. She wanted desperately to say something meaningful to Flannel. But he wanted her not to say it, and she sensed that, too. Still she tried. "I know that I was always special . . ." she began. And that was true. But then his father was special, too, Flannel had realized after his father was dead. Oh, Flannel had known before his father died that Thomas Bonner was different from other men, but when Flannel was growing up he didn't know how different his father was. Flannel was sure that Banyan thought their mother was special, too. And Field was patient with her—Flannel wasn't always—and Field looked after her. Flannel's impatience was too obvious sometimes.

After they left, Flannel went to Houston with Horner and Ellie. Flannel visited his firm's branch office there and pretended that he was conducting some business.

Flannel liked Horner's house. Its deck in back overlooked a deep bayou. He slept in their boys' room, hung with posters of drug-dead rock singers, and got up at sunrise to go out and watch the mockingbirds fussing in the oaks.

Horner took Flannel to the airport. All of his brothers always did things like that for Flannel, and he just accepted their gestures as his due because, after all, he was the one who was always in a hurry. He was the one who was always rushing off on important business.

"Are you happy, Horner?" Flannel asked.

"Sure, Tarzan. Why not? I've just become a partner in one of Texas's mightiest law firms."

"What do you do for fun?"

"Oh, I hunker down beside my shed out in back of the house and watch the cottonmouths play in the muddy water. I can pick my nose at the same time. What do you do for fun?"

Flannel laughed. "I sleep a lot and sometimes I pretend that our past is something I once read about in a novel."

"You always did read too much." Horner turned his car into the lane that would let Flannel out at the Eastern section of Houston's sprawling airport.

They shook hands, and Flannel got his bag off the backseat. "It's been good to see you, Horner. Thanks." He shut the car door and turned away, patting his jacket pocket to see if his plane ticket was there, nervous and apprehensive, the way he always was when he was about to get on a plane.

Then in front of him, rushing the season, walked a plump blond woman in a summer dress, cut low to expose her shoulders and back. She had the beginning of a tan so that the blond hairs on her body were a golden fuzz. That's the way Horner's back had looked when he was a baby, covered with beautiful golden fuzz.

What if, Flannel thought, he caught up to the woman and quickly leaned over and kissed her on the shoulder? "It's all right, miss. Please! Don't yell," he would have to say the instant she turned in surprise, panic on her face. "I was thinking of my baby brother. . . ."

Flannel then would have just about thirty seconds, he figured, to try to explain to her the elusive, confusing, fleeting nature of love—sincerely, convincingly—before she began screaming for the police.

ABOUT THE AUTHOR

Campbell Geeslin grew up in West Texas, was in the Navy during World War II, and earned degrees at Columbia College and the University of Texas. He worked on *The Houston Post* and for the Gannett newspapers before moving to New York as managing editor of *This Week* magazine. He has been editor of The New York Times Syndicate, and for the last five years has worked for Time, Inc., at present on *Life*. He and his wife have three children and live in White Plains, N.Y.